Sensorially Challenged

Volume 1

Allen's Sensory Overload Writing Challenge was conceived by Allen Ashley.

First published December 2017.

You can learn more about Allen's Sensory Overload Writing Challenge and many other writing challenges at:

www.christopherfielden.com

ISBN: 1978498896
ISBN-13: 978-1978498891

DEDICATION

In memory of Bernie 'The Word' Childs.

The Word was a legend of aviation engineering, the father of my friend, James, and the man who came up with the name of the band James and I have played in since 1987.

If you've flown on a Concorde, The Word is the reason the plane stayed in one piece, despite the thrust generated by four Rolls-Royce / Snecma Olympus 593 Mrk610 turbojet engines.

If you've flown on a Boeing 747, he's the reason the wings stayed on.

If you've heard of a band called Airbus, he's the reason it's called Airbus.

He is known as The Word, because he always got the last word on any project he was involved in.

His words of wisdom are greatly missed.

Allen Ashley & Chris Fielden

INTRODUCTION 1 – STOP MAKING SENSE

by Allen Ashley

I'd like to say that I used to be a deadly serious writer until I discovered Christopher Fielden... but that wouldn't be strictly true. I had form with the silly stuff. My poem 'H. P. Lovecraft's Loathly Eldritch Band', anyone?

As a creative writing tutor, I'm always on the lookout for markets and venues for my writers to check out. I knew of Chris Fielden through his 'To Hull And Back' competition, which I had taken to a couple of my groups. Blimey, I probably even signed up for his mailing list as well. When he and Mike Scott Thomson started the Adverb Challenge, that was it, I was hooked. I love writing to restrictions and I particularly like something which pops the po-faced balloon. Yes, writing should seek to say something but it's also good to have a bit of fun with it at other times.

By the time I actually met Chris in the 'real' world – well, Bristol – he had already started his Nonsense Challenge as well, co-editing with Lesley Truchet. I wanted a part of the action and had the not so secret mission to pitch a challenge to him. After a few beers and a lengthy chat about writing groups, judging competitions, being in rock bands, etc., I was raring to go. But what would be the theme or restriction?

In early 2015, I edited a book of science fiction, fantasy and horror stories entitled *Sensorama: Stories of the Senses*. It's a top anthology that is still available from publisher Eibonvale Press. One of the stories got reprinted in a 'Year's Best' book as well. Now, you could say if something is worth doing, it's worth redoing. But this time with not quite such a serious intent.

So the Sensory Writing Challenge was born. I would ask authors to fill their stories with sensory impressions and descriptions. The many ‘How To’ books advise you to be precise and careful when using sensory words or description. “Avoid purple prose,” in common parlance. Thus, in the spirit of these palate-cleansing, vision-clearing, aromatic, eye-watering, velvet touch, not so softly whispered writing challenges our response was: Stuff that: the purpler the better.

And here are the first 100 responses from our authors. Enjoy.

Allen Ashley,

London, September 2017.

INTRODUCTION 2 – START MAKING SENSE

by Chris Fielden

Welcome to the first sensory challenge anthology. This is the fourth book published via the writing challenges run on my website.

The sensory challenge was birthed from the acoustic, aromatic, bright, piquant and viscous mind of Allen Ashley. (See what I did there? Sagacious *and* subtle. I've outdone myself.)

Allen's Sensory Overload Writing Challenge was launched in March 2017. We received our 100th submission in August 2017. Volume 2 is already filling up with some great stories.

The sensory challenge raises awareness of a common rookie writing mistake – the overuse of purple prose. Too much sensory description can make a story too colourful; too complex to digest. It might invoke a feeling of nausea. In turn, that might induce a headache. A cold, damp cloth on one's forehead might–

I'm doing it again. I'll stop. In other news...

I was contacted recently by a fine gent named Allen Stroud (AKA Allen^2), a friend of Allen^1. Allen^2 let me know about an article he'd read in the Basingstoke Observer that reported a Guinness World Record attempt for the most contributing authors published in an anthology. The current world record is 50. The new record attempt is 100.

Allen^2 knew we'd already published a book with 100 contributing authors in it – a legendary tome entitled *Nonsensically Challenged Volume 1* – and suggested we claim the record.

I read the article. It implied that you need to sell

over 1,000 copies of a book to qualify for the record. That's tough to achieve, even with 100 contributing authors spreading the word.

Still, I've contacted Guinness World Records. I've told them about the first nonsense book. And I've also told them about the 81words writing challenge. You can learn more about that on my website:

www.christopherfielden.com/writing-challenges/81words.php

Whether *Nonsensically Challenged Volume 1* is a record contender or not, I've decided to use the 81words writing challenge to try and set a new world record. If we receive 1,000 stories, written by 1,000 authors and release that as a book, that will smash any record. If each author bought one copy, that could get us into the Guinness Book of World Records. Doable, I reckon.

When I hear back from Guinness World Records and know exactly what we need to do to claim the record, I'll start shouting about this epic project more actively. If you'd like to take part, visit the link I mentioned above. We've already received over 120 stories.

OK, enough waffle from me.

Oh, actually, a few last bits of introductory info – the stories in this book are presented in the order they were received. Where supplied, the writer's biography appears with their story. Proceeds from book sales support the fabulous National Literacy Trust.

Chris Fielden,

Brizzle*, October 2017.

** Brizzle is a term used to refer to the city of Bristol, in the United Kingdom, by its residents, Bristolians.*

INTRODUCTION 3

by The National Literacy Trust

The National Literacy Trust in an independent charity that gives disadvantaged children the literacy skills they need to succeed in life. We improve reading, writing, speaking and listening skills in the UK's poorest communities where up to 40% of people have literacy problems that hold them back at every stage of their life.

When children enjoy reading and writing, it has a transformative impact on how well they do at school and in every aspect of their future lives. We are so grateful to the editors, authors and readers of this anthology, whose passion and support will help us to change life stories by giving even more children a route out of poverty.

To find out more about our work, please visit our website:

www.literacytrust.org.uk

ACKNOWLEDGMENTS

Big thanks to Allen Ashley for conceiving and helping me bring the Sensory Challenge to life. You can learn more about Allen here: www.allenashley.com

Thanks to David Fielden for designing the cover of this book and building and maintaining my website. Without him, I'd never have created a platform that allowed the writing challenges I run to be so successful. You can learn more about Dave's website building skills at: www.bluetree.co.uk

Finally, a delicious, colourful, velvety, pungent and, most importantly, very loud, "THANK YOU," to everyone who has submitted their stories, supported this crazy idea and, in turn, raised funds for the National Literacy Trust. At the time of writing, we are already well on the way to 100 stories for *Sensorially Challenged Volume 2*. Without the support of all the writers who submit their stories, this simply wouldn't be possible.

SENSORIALLY CHALLENGED

1: SENSORY SPELL

by Allen Ashley

This was to be a watery experience like no other and Sasha could hardly sleep for impending excitement. Her shower gel had been hand-pressed and packed by above minimum wage earning denizens of the legendary Floral Isles; purchased with two clicks on the internet; depleting her bank balance substantially, but who cared? Because she was worth it.

She squeezed out a medium-sized globule, relishing its soft stickiness on her palm. In some lights it looked red, but as it lathered up the colour was somewhere between rose and tangerine. Hmm, inhale that heavenly aroma of mangoes, guava, hibiscus flower. A flick of the tongue and even its taste was appealing: fruity, not at all artificial.

One sense missing. She clicked her phone to speaker, showered successfully to the pumping beat of Beyoncé's 'Crazy In Love'.

Only the need to dry, dress and head off to work would ever break this paradisiacal sensory spell.

To hell with work. Let's pamper... while her daily water ration lasted.

~

Allen Ashley's Biography

Allen Ashley is the co-originator of the Sensory Challenge project. He is the author or editor of 14 published books including *The Planet Suite* (Eibonvale

Press, 2016). He works as a creative writing tutor with six groups currently on the go.

www.allenashley.com

2: MRS STONE'S ENT APPOINTMENT

by Christopher Fielden

The room stinks of disinfectant. You'd think with the amount of tax my Harold paid over the years they'd be able to afford something more fragrant.

The walls look like a paint factory has vomited on them. Modern art, they call it... Makes me feel queasy.

I look up and see my name in large red letters. Now everyone in the waiting room knows who I am. There's no privacy nowadays.

I lick my lips and taste denture adhesive. It's too minty. How am I supposed to enjoy a cuppa when it feels like I've been force-fed a Polo production plant?

I touch the door handle. It's filthy. With £350,000,000 a week back in the NHS, you'd think they could afford to pay a few cleaners.

The doctor's sitting behind his desk. His mouth's moving.

"What?" I say.

He says something else. Why do young people mumble?

"You'll have to speak up, dear."

He stands and puts something in my ear.

"How's that, Mrs Stone?" he bellows.

"There's no need to shout, dear. I'm not deaf."

~

Christopher Fielden's Biography

Chris writes, runs a humorous short story competition,

plays drums and rides his motorcycle, sometimes to Hull. And back again.

He has recently started running writing challenges and hopes to publish 1,000s of authors in the support of charity.

www.christopherfielden.com

3: GUILTY PLEASURE

by Louise Burgess

Step one of the diet, throw all junk food in the bin.

Easy, right?

However, holding the soft, half-eaten chocolate cake in my chubby pink hands made my mouth water like a bloodhound. Why was the smell of dark chocolate so tempting?

I must resist, although it had cost me £30 at the bakers to buy and I couldn't afford to just toss that money away now, could I?

So, sitting down on the cold wooden kitchen chair, I indulge in a small bite. The instant the moist cake melts in my mouth, with the white frosting covering my lips, I feel pure happiness. Something this heavenly, in three layers of chocolate with a white frosted top, could not be that bad for you. So I take another bite of the calorific forbidden treat.

The door swings open, making me jump out my chair like a guilty two year old, with chocolate covering my mouth and fingers.

~

Louise Burgess's Biography

My first published story was, of course, dedicated to my son, Emmet, but my second has to be dedicated to my amazing husband, Rick, because without him, I would never have the time or energy to write. Thank you.

www.loopybwritingpage.wordpress.com

4: DAWN MUSIC

by Susan Powis

Small stones whisper and shift uneasily beneath half-hearted waves as the unrehearsed choir of seabirds begin to sing in cacophonous dissonance. The wraithlike haar wanders as aimlessly as a contented beachcomber at the edge of the gunmetal sea until a sudden salt-laden zephyr pushes her up the shingle bank. She seeks sanctuary at a beach hut where she clings to the eaves with ephemeral hands. Droplets of moisture weave lacy patterns on their downward glide, stopping momentarily to hang like pearls on a lace-maker's bobbin, the ensuing pattering on the decking adding a syncopated rhythm to the music of the morning.

As the sun's exhalations breathe a hole in the hazy shroud, the haar melts away and the discordant choir falls silent. Landmarks loom out of the milky miasma as the mist rolls away to reveal the blue-on-blue line that demarcates Cambridge sky from Oxford water. As the new day takes its first breath, there follows a satisfying silence broken only by mellifluous birdsong from fragrant hedgerows and sibilant stones shifting with the salty tide.

~

Susan Powis's Biography

Sue Powis, from Birmingham, formerly a Special Needs Teacher and Speech Therapy Assistant. Retired and having the most fun a person can have on their own (thanks TP), apart from jumping up and down in muddy puddles with my granddaughter.

5: DEVELOPING A STRONG STOMACH

by Glynis Ann Downey

I remember those nauseating smells. When I first started nursing, they were hard to deal with. Now, it's easier.

I recall having to learn how to handle it and clear up, no matter how unpleasant the task.

Sometimes, the smell never left me. It seemed to stick to parts of my body, until I got out into the fresh pine wood surrounding the hospital. Trees never smelled so good.

I felt for the patients. It's how I learned to cope. Sometimes, I could see they were embarrassed. They avoided my eye. Touched my hand. Apologised. I reassured them. It was fine. I'd clean them with a smile on my face. It was worse for them.

Considering how a patient must feel was a good lesson. My life in the hospital never seemed as bad after that.

~

Glynis Ann Downey's Biography

I started life in Berkshire. Left home at 18 to start nursing. Finished after 38 years. Also trained as a Psychotherapist. Worked in London.

Now living in the West of Ireland. Started writing some years ago after taking some creative writing courses.

www.facebook.com/glynis.downey

6: SWEET TREAT

by Maggie Elliott

She could almost taste the crisp, melt in the mouth cookies as her eyes scanned the ingredients in the recipe.

Tapping the sieve with the flat of her hand to refine the flour, she felt the dust cloud covering her face. A couple of coughs cleared her throat as the butter plopped into the bowl before the whirring of the mixer beat it into a smooth concoction that smelled of dairy.

The icing sugar produced a silky-smooth texture, but sniffing the vanilla essence before adding caused her eyes to water and her head to recoil.

She felt a blast of heat as she opened the door to slide the mixture into the oven. They smelled delicious.

Once assembled, the sweetness of the biscuit, together with the buttercream and jam filling, almost sent her body into sugar overload.

All she had to decide now was how to consume these delicious Viennese Whirls with the tea she had just poured – dunk and bite or nibble and slurp. Separating them afforded her twice the joy.

~

Maggie Elliott's Biography

Maggie Elliott, originally from Airdrie, is a retired PA living in Oxfordshire and writes purely for pleasure.

She loves animals, particularly cats, listening to holistic music (David Sun, Deuter etc.) and watching comedies.

7: DECOMPOSING

by Dora Bona

He stares with bitterness at his reflection in the silver teapot. Strings of yellowing hair, sparse and greasy, cling to his jaundiced skull. He is withering like the late spring daffodils.

A bowl of food sits untouched on the table. He knows without tasting a morsel that the brackish slop, intended to nourish him, will only attack his resolve like fast acting poison. One hand rests on the cracked surface of the ancient Bible, yet he still feels its leathery newness. He is decaying like a rotten thing.

Fulvid walls, once white and alive, now yawn with tired apathy. His fingers shake as they straddle a smouldering cigarette. He has barely the energy to bring it to his lips. If you lie down you will not be afraid; when you lie down, your sleep will be sweet.

Tendrils of smoke enter his nostrils – hungry maggots scrambling towards his lungs.

Staccato words pierce the silence like ricocheting bullets.

"Dad, for Chrissakes. What have I told you about smoking in the house?"

~

Dora Bona's Biography

Dora has been a freelance writer for 25 years, and puts food on the table by creating marketing material, blogs, commercials and other boring but necessary hack work.

She teaches creative writing classes and writes fiction in her spare time.

www.creativejuicy.com

8: HOT DOGS AND CANDYFLOSS

by Alan Barker

The wind whistled as I crunched across the shingle beach, ozone from the flapping seaweed taking my breath away. I looked up at the empty funfair.

I remembered Easter last year. The blasting sound of pop music drumming in my ears, the oily smell and dull thumps of the bumper cars accompanied by the screams and laughter of their drivers.

I started off the day enticed by the juicy taste of hotdogs covered in fried onions, allowing the hot mustard to dribble down my chin.

Then there was the water chute, where I gripped the car rail tightly as it plunged into the depths, and the loud splash of cold water which drenched me to the skin, so that my T-shirt and shorts clung to me, but soon I dried in the hot afternoon sun.

The *crack, crack* of the rifle range encouraged me to have a go. I won a soft, fluffy, toy rabbit.

I left, grasping my prize whilst enjoying a small cloud of sweet, sticky candyfloss.

~

Alan Barker's Biography

I live in South Wales, a land of many legends. I enjoy writing short plays, stories with a twist and poetry. Living in a Roman town and my love of nature inspire my writing.

9: THE MYSTERY OF THE UBIQUITOUS, SOLITARY SHOE

by Helen Combe

The crunching, gravelly, birdsong filled walk smelled of pungent leaf-mould and insidious mud. Turning my chilly face to the comforting, warming sun, I beheld a shoe swinging by its laces from a telegraph wire. I turned to my boyfriend, smelling the sultry musk of aftershave and the piquant, lemony zing of hair gel mixed with the earthy reek of his creaking wax jacket.

"What is the mystery of these ubiquitous, solitary shoes?" I asked, as my foot suddenly slipped and, aghast and disbelieving, I toppled sideways into the freezing canal. The icy fluid slapped my face, bubbled and roared in my ears, stung my nose and froze my mouth with bitter, swampy silt. The world was engulfed in benumbing darkness as I sank.

A strangling, tightening round my throat was followed with upward rushing as my boyfriend hauled me gasping to the surface and flapping onto the towpath.

My left foot felt wrong, light and loose yet numbingly cold.

I found that I was at one with the mystery of the ubiquitous solitary shoe.

~

Helen Combe's Biography

Helen is a member of Solihull Writers and was published

in the prestigious *To Hull And Back Short Story Anthology 2016*. Her next proudest moment was being voted Ruler of the Universe at a sci-fi con as Servalan from *Blake's 7*.

www.facebook.com/HelenCombeWriter/

10: SMOKE

by Dee Tilsley

The acrid smoke filled Shona's nostrils, cloying, choking. *Why didn't I open the window?* she thought frantically. *Why did I choose tonight to burn it*? Oh to feel the soft breeze on her face, to breathe deep the sweet smell of the air, heavy with honeysuckle on the other side of this dirty, distorted glass. To be running through the meadow of sweet, fresh mown grass that she knew lay just out of reach.

Too late. Too late to stop the bright, sudden glare that had lit her scared but determined face in the mirror. Far, far too late to replace the rough, scratchy, sulphurous box of matches back into the old wooden drawer. Too late for any chance of redemption, of reprieve.

She heard the wood of the stairs creak, felt the tremor in the floorboards as the heat warmed her hands and the smoke brought tears to her eyes. Too late.

It was so unfair. She shuddered with fear as she heard the eldritch screech...

"Shona, are you smoking in there again?"

~

Dee Tilsley's Biography

Mum of three, Dawn juggles a full-time job and cares for her family whilst trying to keep the creative little grey cells doing star jumps. With a hop, skip and a jump, she falls majestically into a quivering heap every evening.

11: BULLY

by Eddie Regory

Rocheet squirmed out from under me and jumped into a Bruce Lee stance, brushing his thumb over his nose. He brought his head down and charged at me like a raging bull, knocking me backward into the ground.

"Ah, you bit my arm," I yelled. I leveraged my hands under his chest and, with all my might, pushed him over, jamming my fingers into his eyes.

He begged me to stop, but I wouldn't. Then he got loose again. I tackled him to the ground and pounded his face. As Rocheet lay there protecting himself, an evil grin formed on his face.

Rocheet pleaded, "I quit."

"You promise?"

"I promise."

I jumped off, hoping it was over.

"I lied," Rocheet exclaimed.

I shouted, "Don't you ever give up?" Anger bubbled up from my stomach.

A teacher rushed over and shouted, "Stop it," forcing her skinny arms between us as the blood from my arm trickled over her hands. The teacher snatched me by my arm and pulled me aside.

~

Eddie Regory's Biography

I'm originally from New York City but consider myself a Portland, Oregon native. I like all movies including the stupid ones (life's too short not to try them), going on long bike rides, dogs and great conversation.

www.amazon.com/Wallace-Park-Eddie-Regory-ebook/dp/B00A7BSFS6/

12: A DIFFERENT VACATION

by Sivan Pillai

I didn't know what startled me out of my slumber – the cacophony of birds, the barking of dogs, the mooing of cows, shafts of sunlight filtered through the foliage of giant trees entering through the windows or the aroma of food wafting in from the kitchen.

Soon after sundown, a pall of darkness had engulfed the area, but after a while faint, twinkling stars had become visible through gaps in the quick-moving clouds in the sky, followed by an infant moon.

While I lay tossing in bed, jackals had seemed to howl from just outside the windows.

When I returned from a tingling bath in the icy, fast-flowing stream, the dining table was laden with steaming food. The spicy dishes made my eyes water, but the sweet and sour fruits brought some solace.

Father, worried that the internet was taking too much of my time, had asked me to spend the vacation with my grandparents in a village that had no internet, cell-phone, television or uninterrupted electric supply.

Thank you, Dad.

~

Sivan Pillai's Biography

Sivan Pillai is a retired professor of English from Gujarat Agricultural University, Navsari, India. His stories have been published by *Flash Fiction Magazine*, 101 Words and others. He lives in Navsari, India.

13: PARADISE MISLAID

by Norman Longworth

I clamber reluctantly from my bed, mind still cluttered with sleep, and peer through the French windows. It's still there – that brainless magnificent mountain presiding spectacularly over its fiefdom in the valley below. 9,000 feet of snow-capped rock standing guard over my land, my house, me.

"Good morning, your majesty," I say.

I open the window – oh dear, not sunshine again. It's March. Winter for goodness sake.

The sounds and smells of a French rural landscape attack my fogbound senses. Tractors passing, nightingales ending their night-long symphony – they must be completely exhausted. Kept me delightfully awake last night.

Peaches, pears, cherries, in full-painted blossom. I can almost taste the pesticides they pour over the poor buds. Shouldn't be allowed.

I stagger downstairs. Breakfast time. Not that stupid muesli again. Tastes like sand and gravel. But the croissants are pure musk.

From the balcony I see Eus, my village perché, houses cascading down the hillside in a crazy Dali-esque waterfall.

And this is Paradise? Humbug.

Might change my mind when I wake up.

~

Norman Longworth's Biography

Born doubtful paradise of Bolton, now real paradise South France. Ex-labourer, bank clerk, statistician, teacher, salesman, research scientist, manager, university professor, writer etc. Will retire at 150 and achieve it by 22nd century.

Daily ambition to create a better tomorrow, but since tomorrow never comes, is destined to wander forever in liberal purgatory, always en route and never getting there.

14: A SENSATE EXPERIENCE

by Lesley Truchet

The sight of it activated my salivary glands. My heartbeat accelerated. This was my first time.

I listened to the words of guidance.

"Smell it."

I closed my eyes and breathed in the moist pungent aroma.

"Touch it."

With my fingertips I lightly caressed its cool velvety length.

"Taste it."

I closed my eyes and allowed my tongue to glide languidly over the smooth surface, finally taking the end into my warm mouth, savouring the thick creamy substance.

Today I'm a famous movie star, but I've never forgotten my first ever moment in front of a camera, making a TV commercial for a chocolate iced lolly.

~

Lesley Truchet's Biography

Lesley Truchet has been writing for several years and has a number of short stories, articles and poems published on paper and on the internet. She is currently writing her first novel.

15: WALK

by Marilyn Thompson

Wind buffets my body, threatening to hurl me from the ribbon of tramped earth stretched along the top of the dyke. Clouds weigh on shuttered beach houses, pressing them into a landscape greyed by winter. Rain slants down. Stings my face. Inveigles its way through the gap between waterproofs and walking shoes. I lean into the rising storm. Cold drills through layers of clothes to chill my bones. Rain turns to sleet. I can taste the bitterness of it on my tongue. Waves leap the breakers, roar their fury along the Sea Wall and recoil into the Wash as if afraid of the land.

I pause momentarily, tempted by a huddle of trees below, then keep on walking. In this weather, movement is life. To stop is to stop forever.

Concentrate. Place one foot in front of the other. Feel the ground beneath my feet. Heel, toe. Try not to stumble and fall in the fading light. I am old but if I can do this, then I ain't dead yet.

~

Marilyn Thompson's Biography

I write contemporary fantasy influenced by history and fairy tales. I am working on two novels set in imaginary English landscapes: *Maiden Eve* and *Waterside*. I have an MA in Creative Writing from Anglia Ruskin University in Cambridge.

16: THE BALLAD OF THE MASQUERADE BALL

by Betty Hattersley

King Henry the eighth of England,
Loved to frolic and also demand,
He created the Masque for people of court,
To cover one's face and disguise, was his thought.
Hidden behind their costumes,
As the harpsichord's sound filled the room,
Musicians would play for jesters to dance,
At the Mediaeval Masque they'd go in a trance.
Beautiful gowns of velvet and gold,
King Henry had eyes for ladies so bold.
Gents in silk britches, with wigs piled up high,
Mead flowing in goblets, no person was shy.
An evening of music, laughter and fun,
Their identity hidden till evening was done.
A pig roast prepared for folks to enjoy,
Quail eggs with chicken and venison pie.
Passions aroused at the Masquerade ball,
Henry would choose his maids from them all.
Whilst watching and choosing from his throne where he sat,
Through too much indulgence, the king became fat.

~

Betty Hattersley's Biography

I've been writing for many years and have had numerous poems and short stories published in anthologies, newspapers, calendars and magazines.

I've written a small book (yet to be published) about the funny side of my outside catering days.

17: SOMETHING OLD

by Danielle Dayney

With gentle force, she pulled the tattered sheet off the ornate dresser. A cloud of dust plumed into the air, swirling around the wooden beauty. It was full of curves: soft to look at, but hard to the touch as she traced her fingers across each hand-carved detail.

She imagined her grandmother's perfumes that were once displayed upon it: potent and flowery. Its finish had been worn from it being opened and closed, battered and bumped, over the years. It was her plan to give it life once more.

She opened the smooth plastic container of chalk paint, and a new, clean smell filled the space. Gentle brush strokes covered each camber and cranny with paint. Once the paint dried, she used the coarse edge of her sanding block and found her rhythm. Sweat dripped down her forehead and onto her temples as she distressed and sanded each edge to perfection.

Using a cloth, she buffed and shined the sticky wax until smooth, then stopped to stand and marvel that something old was new again.

~

Danielle Dayney's Biography

Danielle is sometimes a blogger, usually a writer, and always Mom. You can find her chasing kids and furbabies somewhere in Virginia, or at:

www.danielledayney.com

18: PANIC (ATTACK) AT THE DISCO

by Paige Vest

The murmur of concertgoers grows louder as roadies perform sound checks. Fans rush toward the stage and I realise that we've been separated. My eyes search but I don't see you.

Strangers jostle me, stepping on my toes while seeking better positions. I feel my heart pounding. I'm anxious without you beside me.

I cross my arms and dig my fingernails into my flesh hard enough to bruise. Pain grounds me and I seek escape from the suffocating mob.

The lights go down and the crowd roars, pressing forward, dragging me along. I'm sightless in the dark and smells assault me as I struggle to escape the gridlock: perfume, beer, sweat... the cloying aroma of marijuana smoke.

Sudden spotlights blind me as the band takes the stage. Gigantic speakers assault with sound which pounds my eardrums and thumps against my chest.

The shouts of delirious fans drown out my sobbing. Fists pump the air and an elbow hits my tear-streaked face. I taste blood and nausea rises.

I can't find you anywhere.

Panic consumes me.

~

Paige Vest's Biography

Paige Vest has loved stories since childhood when she

first visited Middle Earth and Narnia. She tells stories today to quiet the voices in her head.

Paige is currently at work on the second novel of a YA trilogy.

www.writinginthedark.blog

19: SEASON'S END

by Melony Boseley

Rose sat on the back patio and ignored the harsh tones reverberating from inside.

Auburn foliage cascaded onto the verdant landscape. The wind carried the smells of grilled meats with it. Joy and splashes echoed in the air.

The warmth of summer had not yet passed, but the chill of autumn had not begun.

Her tiny feet dangled from the stained deck. In her voice there was a melody of her own making, marking tempo with each swing of the leg.

It was the perfect moment.

One that she would later come to realise marked the end of her childhood.

~

Melony Boseley's Biography

Melony is an American (correction: Texan) living in Australia. She can be found writing on her blog, has been published in *Sammiches & Psych Meds*, and recently contributed to a first place win of the Team Writer's Games with Writer's Workout.

www.melonyboseley.wordpress.com

20: BEDROOM ALONE

by Sandra Orellana

Joy came out through her bedroom window: a farewell to her room. Her neighbour saw her, but at that moment they both vanished.

The bedroom stayed; a space with items. A mirror reflecting comfort for a static noise TV. A lonely bed, scattered with written papers left behind for anyone to read, to be used and feel what used to be felt. The room's colours gave it joy for other items to encompass the energy and spirit. Smells of roses beside her bedside table. The cup of coffee and left over chocolate bars made a worthy scent for the lonely room. A Bible opened on Proverbs 24:4: "By knowledge the rooms are filled with all precious and pleasant riches." Walls: no one can hear the sound of a dog scratching the door to be open. The light from an open window shining through, bringing the outdoor breeze. Papers were like heartbroken souls left behind. The room frozen as if waiting for the creator of Heaven and Earth to put this time back to life.

~

Sandra Orellana's Biography

Sandra Orellana is an American amateur writer who was born in El Paso, Texas, on the border of México.

Her passions are tennis, writing and reaching out to the most in need. She spends her time living in México City and San Miguel Allende.

Her book, *Arch Of Surprises,* is being published by Lighthouse Publishing.

21: TWO LITTLE LINES

by Donna-Louise Bishop

She flinched as the roll-up, which had stuck to her lip, ripped off a peeling of red-stained skin. Its shade was Sunset Lust. At least that's what the shop assistant had told her earlier that day. Now she thought it looked cheap. Less lust, more lame.

Vibrations from the conversations and trance music blaring out in her flat wiggled their way outside and onto the balcony where she stood alone, shivering in her strapless dress. It was mild for New Year's Eve, but that didn't mean it wasn't cold.

In one fluid motion she gulped the last of her wine and took one final drag of her cigarette, letting it sting the now raw patch of skin. Wedging it between her thumb and middle finger, she flicked the butt into the darkness below.

She hadn't planned to do the test until tomorrow morning. *Ignorance is bliss*, she thought. But now those two pink lines had changed everything. And despite the fear she felt, she knew next year would be the start of something wonderful.

~

Donna-Louise Bishop's Biography

Donna-Louise Bishop is a freelance journalist and creative writer from Norfolk, UK. Mum to three noisy boys, she enjoys writing microfiction and is also working on her first novel. More of her work can be found on

her blog:
www.newshoundnovelist.wordpress.com

22: NO BRAIN-PICKERS FOR HER

by Glen Donaldson

The late afternoon sky oozes through the mullioned bay windows in an optimistic, lady-like shade of grey. Inside, Beryl listens to the pop of unseasoned firewood as it makes the final shift and crumbles into embers. Without warning, a foul odour drifts from the kitchen. Next moment, her date – the exotically named Avocado – pushes his way through a shuttered swinging door holding, waiter-style, a silver tray brimming with food.

Beryl licks her fleshy lips and grabs a handful of oily hors d'oeuvres.

"Can I pick your brain?" asks Avocado, sitting down opposite her in a mahogany chair with cherubs chiselled into the sides.

In apt response, Beryl belches operatically, then collects her oatmeal coloured overcoat and leaves. She'd always loathed the expression 'Can I pick your brain?' and for a dedicated wordophile like her, it was a deal breaker.

No brain-pickers for me, was the affirmation that looped through her phrase-coiffured head as she strode onto the avenue. Determination drove her on. Determination to find the right words and the one who could speak them.

~

Glen Donaldson's Biography

Glen Donaldson enjoys eating peeled grapes and

activated almonds and knows how literary that probably sounds. He blogs at Scenic Writer's Shack:
www.goosefleshsite.wordpress.com

23: THE FIRST NOTE

by Nicole Loh

The lights were blinding. It hurt her eyes as she stood on the polished wooden floor of the stage. She couldn't see the faces of her audience and her shoulders relaxed. Her fingers were not quivering and shaking, and her heart stopped thumping, just enough for her to hear the little murmurs coming from behind her.

She filled her lungs with air that tasted of air conditioning and loosened her grip around the violin's neck. She turned her head. A blur of browns, silvers and blacks. The violins, cellos, trumpets and flutes. They dressed in a sea of black and white. Her red, flowing gown that fluttered like a butterfly stood out, much like a sore thumb. The attention made her shoulders tenser, but still she nodded, ignoring the growing lump in her throat. They took their positions and awaited her cue. They were ready for her to take the audience on a musical journey.

She raised her violin and played the first note. It rang through the halls and resonated in their hearts.

~

Nicole Loh's Biography

Malaysian. Lover of all things art. Nicole has chosen the written word as her medium to bring her brand of art into the world, despite the harsh realities of unpaid bills. Her favourite subjects include cultural identities, feminism, and music.

Find Nicole on Twitter: @nicoleloh_

24: PLACEHOLDER

by Michelle Konov

In the end, I was nothing more than a scapegoat, he thought as he glanced around, taking in the bright red lights flashing erratically throughout the building. The deep, ashy scent of flames wafted up from the ground floor and he wondered, not for the first time, if they had really thought they could kill him so easily.

Creeping slowly forward toward the window, he kept out of sight as much as possible. The smooth grains of the windowsill under his hands were a clear juxtaposition to the ragged flames rising behind him.

Shrill sirens pierced through the air, firefighters and policemen already arriving on the scene, eyeing the ruin of a building as if displeased.

He moved to the rear of the building. Thankfully, it was empty of both cars and people. As he tumbled through the third floor window and made a particularly fine landing on a lamppost nearby, he gave a thought to revenge.

They always said it was a dish served cold, but he liked it red hot. And preferably on fire.

~

Michelle Konov's Biography

No author biography supplied.

25: PARADISE

by Brandon Brown

The boat had docked.

The first thing I could feel was the cool breeze drifting through the winds, impacting my face.

The sound of loud cries from the flocking seagulls above welcomed us. The ramp was secured with a loud clink. With that, people rushed over to secure their place in the queue that was forming.

I was first. I'd been waiting for what felt like forever. It was my right. I'm sure others felt this way, but I was me, not them. I picked up my bags. They were heavy, but I managed to get a porter to help me. He struggled, but tried not to show it.

Crash.

I landed on my bed. It was pristine and fresh, the bedsheet clearly washed and prepared that morning. All I could think of was how the next two weeks could turn out. I looked out over my balcony and my senses heightened. The view and aroma of the food from below me was incredible.

~

Brandon Brown's Biography

No author biography supplied.

26: SENSUAL WARFARE

by Jack Caldwell-Nichols

I felt as though I could taste the aroma, such was the attack on my senses. It was almost offensive. No, it *was* offensive. My eyes were watering. Offensive. Or maybe it was the pain in my stomach causing the tears. What was that? I started worrying desperately about arranging an appointment with good old Doctor Green. Perhaps she could check my olfactory nerve?

Finally, my mother left. Goodness gracious – her new perfume from her new boyfriend, the one with the new flashy red car. Mum jumped in and didn't even bother to wave goodbye. The sight of the flashy red number speeding off into impending retirement was... was it a hernia? It could be a hernia. I remembered hearing a man complaining of having a hernia, describing the experience as a 'darn nuisance'.

What a beautiful day. The sun shone with dizzying brightness. A bird graciously flew over me, and I looked on in awe. Then I looked at my shoulder and saw bird poo.

It was time to buy a nice new car.

~

Jack Caldwell-Nichols' Biography

Hailing from the hills, high in the North beyond Hadrian's Wall, comes myself, Jack Caldwell-Nichols. A lover of the craft, taking inspiration from classic British comedy such as *Red Dwarf* to Stephen King's novels. I'll leave you to judge...

27: A PAIR OF EGRETS

by Ellie Bignall

A knifing peppermint wind struck the fields with an explosion of invisible silver; air trickled between every sugared leaf and skated on iced whorls of a petrified brook. The feeble butter sun shivered between iron clouds in a pale mirror sky. Ghosts of a thickly spicy autumn hung silently in the air, suspended like jubilant icicles in mockery of thudding fallen apples and skeleton leaves; a sparkling tapestry of movement and stillness in muted silks and silver thread.

The photographer's luck seemed finally to be turning; the pair of egrets he'd been waiting so long for had decided to nest early, and the burning iciness of the morning had dissuaded hikers from bruising the fields with their greasy chocolate boots.

He'd been tracking for perhaps two hours when he stumbled over a frosted wicker basket thrown carelessly on the earth, dislodged by his churlish shoe. The delicate air was split by a cry. The photographer spun. Far from the mournful sob of a bird, this was the stone grey wail of a baby.

~

Ellie Bignall's Biography

No author biography supplied.

28: SENSES OF LOVE

by Hema Nataraju

I saw him for the first time after the football game the other day. Adrenaline-pumped voices boomed in the showers, but they melted into the billowing steam the moment my eyes rested on his face.

A calm overcame me, a serenity that kneeling before God in a little temple on the hills brings. His eyes were pools of cool water to a thirsty traveller walking through the desert. His sweaty, tanned skin probably tasted like sea-salt chocolate truffles. On cold Netflix-and-chill nights, his muscular, hairy arms must feel like a blanket of warm angora.

Every pore of my body wanted to be close to him.

A scrunched towel hit my head from the back, snapping me out of my reverie. “What’s the matter, Danny boy? You gay for the new guy?” The pack of cackling hyenas walked away.

I wish they had waited for my answer. Love looks angelic, smells and tastes like Grandma’s baking, sounds like violins and fireworks and always feels like coming home.

Why then, is mine any different from theirs?

~

Hema Nataraju’s Biography

Hema is a San Francisco based writer whose stories have appeared in *Chicken Soup for the Soul, The Sunlight Press,* and *The Aerogram.* When she’s not writing, you'll find her drinking copious amounts of coffee and blogging at:

www.hemas-mixedbag.com

29: UNDER A VELVET SKY FROSTED WITH SPARKLING STARS

by Margaret Edwards

The deck rail was blissfully cool and shiny against her cheek. The mellow Merlot coated her throat with inky, plummy liquorice.

Romantic setting, huh? Sadly no; this was the Caen – Portsmouth ferry and her annual booze run. She slurped again.

Footsteps; squeaky shoes approaching, accompanied by a bitter stench of sweat and... something ripely pungent?

Oh hell, she thought. That creep in the French supermarket who'd cornered her by the deli counter and asked her what 'Camembert' was in French.

"Fancy meeting you again." His voice was oily, sneering. "I've got the cheese," (so that was the smell), "and you've got the wine – could be some party." His wet mouth suddenly came slobbering down like a cabbage-fuelled slug. Instinctively she sprang onto the rail and jumped.

Above her, the delighted shrieks of gulls, purposeful shouts from the crew diving in and one baffled whinnying face.

Pressed, caressed by the waves; so tenderly slapped and wrapped, rolled, folded round as in silky foil, beribboned with seaweed like a miraculous present. "But not for you, creep." She smiled.

~

Margaret Edwards' Biography

Writer from age seven, until 30-year gap for absorbing family and job. Now work-free and urgently trying to make up for lost time. Minor poetry prizes and publication, now infatuated with the Short Story but still grovelling in shortlist anterooms.

30: A TALL TALE

by Mike Scott Thomson

...last night I drank one bottle of syrupy saccharine luminous turquoise alcopop and now I have a million clanging chiming bonging bells peeling between my ears so I stagger to the kiosk and croak through my scratchy gravelly vermillion-hued oesophagus, "Tall Americano," and the barista asks, "Medium, large?" and I think, *good, none of those stupid sizes here,* so I say, "Medium," and she pours me a coffee then another and hands both over then says, "Two Americano, five pounds," and I think, *Drat,* but I'm too British to return one so I pay and carry them one in each hand onto the train and think, *well, waste not want not,* so I take a sniff and they're peaty earthy caramelly chestnutty and I take a sip and oof they're gloopy treacly grand-piano-lands-on-head STRONG, but I finish them both and now I can't stop yammering and my heart's going boompety-boom like a billion-piece timpani orchestra and people are edging away and...

Thank goodness I didn't ask for Venti.

~

Mike Scott Thomson's Biography

Mike Scott Thomson's short stories have been published by journals, anthologies and have won the occasional award, including first prize in Chris Fielden's inaugural To Hull And Back competition.

Based in south London, he works in broadcasting.

31: FLY TIPPING AT THE LATE NIGHT FRIED CHICKEN OUTLET

by Martin Strike

The blue light and lazy hum of the Zappo electric fly killer on the wall may be irresistible to you, bluebottle, but death with a spark isn't all it's cracked up to be. Beats flypaper, mind. Everyone hates bright yellow – it's tacky. And sticky. Land there and you'd have time to write your obituary before your drawn-out death – if only your hands weren't glued by the glue you'd flown into. Stuck fast, you could watch your ungunked compatriots poised on lumps of pink, raw meat, only lifting to air should cigarette ash flick from the man slicing burger buns on the same counter.

What is the last thing that goes through your mind before you hit a windscreen, or you're bound in web and feeling the vibrations of the spider coming down-thread? Maybe you'd recall your wriggling maggoty childhood, or happy times spent rubbing your hands, feet soothed on a soft, aromatic turd?

Buzz off now, bluebottle. Fly to choose the death you favour, letting me sit, quite drunk, my meal to savour.

~

Martin Strike's Biography

Cloned by renegade prawns from a bulging consignment of ripe avocados, Martin is an essential ingredient in Seventies starters and face packs. A source

of carotenoids and packed with vitamins, he still finds time to post daft stories on:
www.thenewburyshortstoryteller.wordpress.com

32: MOTTO REMEMBERED

by Michael Rumsey

He stopped opposite Albany Park. A touch on his car horn may have caught attention and elicited a merry wave, but it was currently subdued. Nevertheless, here was a blast from the past.

Tent canvas fluttered gently, guy ropes sat steadfastly taut. A sight for sore eyes, especially if you stood directly in the path of drifting smoke. It wafted lazily towards him to deliver the mouthwatering aroma of frying. A reassuring crackle of spark-filled dry twigs, the spit and sizzle of big thick skin-splitting sausages. Billy cans and tin mugs clicked distantly, patiently waiting for the lip-smacking promise of palatable delights. Sunlight bounced off a gurgling stream where uniformed figures scooped and splashed.

Elated, he surveyed the scene and recalled, as a boy, carefully packing his kit bag for camping weekends. Items ticked off, ready for any eventuality, in line with the Boy Scout motto.

How appropriate he should encounter this exciting atmospheric pageant today, when he was en route to Powell's garage to get his beep repaired.

~

Michael Rumsey's Biography

Michael has had an appetite for writing for some time now. Not seeing clearly where to submit at first, he heard of and touched upon a certain well known website.

These days he sniffs out every opportunity and challenge, sometimes sensitively.

33: FIRST IMPRESSIONS OF AFRICA

by Jennifer Chislett

Nairobi burst upon me in a riot of colour and sound. Bougainvillea tumbling over fences in dazzling colours of purple and scarlet; jacaranda trees along the road foaming with mauve blossom. African women in brightly coloured traditional kangas, babies tucked into the back, swaying along the streets, shopping balanced on their heads.

Cars and taxis hooted, lorries full of men all singing in unison rattled along the roads; spicy aromas from street stalls assaulted my nose and made my mouth water. The feel of the sun on my skin caressing me with warmth, and occasionally a light breeze to temper it was a delightful sensation, having come from a grey and chilly England.

The taste of wonderful drinks, from fruits cut and squeezed as I waited, slaked my thirst whilst wandering along in this new and fascinating world. This vibrant place was to be my home for the next few years and I couldn't wait to experience all it could show me.

~

Jennifer Chislett's Biography

I travelled widely overseas due to my late husband's job. Am now retired with many happy memories. In the past I have written stories for children, some of which were published.

34: THE ROOM

by Jack Probyn

It was dark. Too dark. He didn't know how he got here. But when he woke, the only light that filled the room was the heavy blanket of harsh, fluorescent white that encompassed his mind.

It was painful. Too painful. His skull throbbed with the repetitive beat of his racing heart. Thud thud. Thud thud. Thud thud.

It was cold. Too cold. A delicate wintry breeze swam over the curves and contours of his body. Half his skin rose in protest as the air hugged him tightly, with his nipples leading the attack.

Why was he half naked?

He didn't know. Where was he?

He didn't know.

He struggled to open his eyes, ignoring the pain that ensued. A solitary candle, placed on a large, uneven stone, flickered and danced carelessly in the air. It was aromaless, save for the acrid smell of corrosive chemical and decaying flesh.

The rest of the room was empty, except for tiny rivulets of water weaving down the walls.

Fear grappled him. A figure of death advanced.

~

Jack Probyn's Biography

Jack Probyn is the author of the new and exciting Detective Jake Tanner crime thriller series. The first instalment in the series, *An Unlikely Betrayal,* is available in stores now.

www.jackprobynbooks.com

35: SIMBA

by Karen Vernon

WOOLF.

I wish you would go back to sleep.

WOOLF.

I smell old dog, I hear your tail thumping against the floor.

I pat your head and scruff your crumpled ears. My company is all you want and there is little time left for us; I willingly forego sleep.

I sit with you and run my hands over your fur, the colour of deserts and sunsets, as soft as a rabbit. The ridge runs down your spine like ornate trim on a once fashionable garment.

I remember when I found you; a tiny, crying puppy with breath that smelled like toast. It was late at night, 16 years ago. Much has changed and you stayed by my side for all those years.

But you can no longer follow me.

I sit with you until your tail stops wagging, the light has faded from your eyes, your body has gone cold.

My coffee tastes bitter as the sun rises. I watch birds collect the hair you shed to line their nests.

~

Karen Vernon's Biography

No author biography supplied.

36: INSPECTOR SINGH AT THE SEASIDE

by Ian Tucker

A cooling gust brushed the hairs on his arms, sending light tingles into his skin. It flicked the loose silk of his shirt against his chest and carried salt and fish and the petroleum and wood odour of boats up his nose. His sinuses throbbed with an ache which was more discomfort than pain and his tongue tasted of grit and stale mould from the long night of bad coffee.

The island's last nightclub boomed bass notes which shook the cold steel of the pier's handrail. He bit into the samosa Sanchez had brought him and felt the spice burn his lips and tongue before the warm sweet ghee smothered it. Below, wavelets rustled on the beach, muttering as they overturned loose pebbles, drawing transient white contours at the edge of the still, black and purple sea. High above, the moon glowed blue.

The breeze died back and the cloying smell of perfume and blood from the twisted body at his feet engulfed him again. Its vibrant, multi-coloured sari was spattered with maroon stains.

~

Ian Tucker's Biography

Ian Tucker is a hopeless amateur who writes for fun and so his wife thinks he's busy. There is lots of rubbish by him at:

www.tilebury.com

37: OCEANA

by Cosima Armstrong

My peaceful abode is deep down in the ocean, where I listen to the singing of my graceful companions above me. There used to be very few disruptions. But those tiresome beings who live above the sea tip all sorts of things and ugly noises into it. I can smell their detritus.

They call me a sea monster. But I am beautiful, long and sleek, my jewelled armour illuminating the darkness, as I swish through the silken waters caressing my body. Sometimes I surface and fly high where I see all the Earth with its beauties and miseries.

I used to eat, and can still remember how scrumptious a nice fat sea bass or salmon tasted. They didn't like being eaten. I evolved and stopped eating and found that I didn't need to.

Humans think they've seen me. Not true, I just live in their dreams in the form of half-forgotten legends.

Me, and my melodious companions will still be here, when they, and their commotions, are gone, forever.

~

Cosima Armstrong's Biography

Hooray, the New York Drapers Guild awarded me first prize in August. Chris Fielden's encouraging messages to us all kept me writing, so now I feel doubly blessed and happy. Love writing, haven't written much, but now I shall renew my efforts.

38: BURGER AND THE EMPATHY

by Vaibhav Rathi

I was about to take a hefty burger, as I like to enjoy some junk food every once in a while during the cold season, when I saw a dog wagging its tail heavily and shivering. It was searching for some food, certainly, but I chose to ignore it because it's a regular thing to perceive on the streets of India.

The aroma of soy sauce was getting into my nostrils. I was just being impatient, my mind was drifting across my craving and the dog's hunger.

I took money out of my pocket. I saw a vagrant girl was feeding the dog from the food that wasn't sufficient, even for her. Then she covered the dog with her little blanket and sat beside it. I may have money, but not the heart of that beautiful girl.

I felt guilty so I bought two burgers and walked to the girl. I gave one to the dog and the other to the girl, that little girl who taught me empathy.

~

Vaibhav Rathi's Biography

Assistant professor of plant drug medicines in Uttarakhand, India.

39: SOME ADVICE IS BETTER FOLLOWED

by Tristan Bolton

I awake, staring directly at a very blue sky.

Gradually, I become aware of someone speaking, but I'm feeling a bit bewildered as I'm not currently sure where I am.

"Are you alright, sir?" I hear an unfamiliar but none-the-less sincere voice ask.

"I'm not sure," is all I can truthfully reply. I feel dizzy and the extreme warmth of the day is beginning to make its presence known. I push my hands into the succulent grass beneath me and draw a deep breath, pulling in its freshly cut aroma intermingled with that of traffic fumes and the freshly brewed chai I've been kindly presented with. Its sweet taste starts my reboot.

I should be on a coach, I remember now, that one, over there, the Volvo with the air conditioning. I tentatively pull myself up, assisted by a couple of concerned helpers.

"Are you alright?" I'm asked again.

I am, and I tell them so, but I think perhaps in future I should do as suggested and keep myself adequately hydrated.

~

Tristan Bolton's Biography

I've never been one for self-promotion.

40: BACK

by Yvonne Mallett

"She's back."

She hears the words. Just. They fade, drowned by the seeming-slap of seashore sounds upon the sand.

Again, "She's back." The voice – Male? Female?

Where has she been? She feels cold, body numbed, trembling yet trying to be still.

Merciful anaesthesia thins like fog. Mind and body sense the dizziness.

Then, as the haze upon the mind retreats, again the voice, "She's back."

Where has she been? The question slips from focus in the sharp smell of disinfectant.

Blunt tools probe and thrust to bruise her body.

Now she understands, and certainty prompts recall.

She has been where smiles from those once loved, though not seen for half a lifetime, have touched her, their hands and words so gentle. Their love once nourished her, held her close, warmed her.

Now she looks to find them, tries to speak, tries to hear.

But still she hungers and is chilled.

"You made it," says the voice.

"Oh, send me back," she sobs.

~

Yvonne Mallett's Biography

I always wanted to write and worked my way through

news reporting into advertising and marketing in a writing role. I’ve done quite a bit of freelance magazine writing and once had a play on Radio 3. Now it’s all short stories. I love them.

41: INDELIBLE

by John Wilks

Marauding monkeys screeching and clattering across a corrugated iron roof; three cows with bony, protruding haunches shuffling along a cooling beach, silhouetted against a shimmering orange sunset; a hunchbacked chai-wallah shouting along the cockroach-infested corridor of a train; the insistent call to prayer before dawn, haunting a skyline of air-conditioning units and satellite dishes; the cumin-sizzle of dal fry and chana masala; the fetid squalor of bloated dead rats and stinking cow-dung next to pavement children in rags squatting to sort plastic from cardboard; the taste of scorched naan flecked with ashes straight from the flaming tandoor; the heady, bitter seductiveness of cashew nut feni liqueur; a faded 10 rupee note that pleads a history of a thousand hands; a swishing coconut palm breeze that caresses bare skin flirtatiously.

I've tipped the sand from my trainers, swallowed the last anti-malarial tablet and stopped practising head-wobbles in the bathroom mirror, but, like a love-bite, like a hang-over, like an earworm, like scent on a pillow, like raw chilli on a fingertip, Goa just won't fade away.

~

John Wilks's Biography

John Wilks taught English in inner London for over 30 years before completing the MA in Creative and Life

Writing at Goldsmiths. He is currently working on a collection of stories about men, boys and school. He lives in Greenwich.

42: HUNGRY HEATHER

by L A Moylan

The black bog burns my cheeks a brittle blue. The hungry heather seems to feed on my every step and rain torpedoes my eyes like spikey spores, sharply pulling me on.

I feel her hand somewhere in the future, searching for me at night across the static sheets. Her laughter like spring daffodils, how I ache for the warmth of her teething mouth and sun warm cheek. I can almost smell the milk on her fragile baby breath.

The crow's cry knocks me present, my mind mummy sore. The gnarled knuckles of the edge beckon me closer with constant craggy hunger. I see him now, watching TV, slurping up tepid gravy as it drips on his greying Brillo pad beard. His wide fingers, finger the worn buttons to bring him to a wide-eyed state of telly unconscious.

I recall the warmth of her brushed cotton back and I breathe in the comfort of her neck. I'm so cold, the wind pushes me forth with an icicle palm, and it gently lulls me over.

~

L A Moylan's Biography

Linda is a singer and songwriter, whose lyrical narrative is influenced by the authors, poets, playwrights and artists who inform the strong storytelling aspect of her songwriting. She can be found foraging in old men's

pubs and here:
www.lindaem.co.uk

43: FADING

by Fiona Jeeves

Although twists of air were scented with pine, it was the dry touch of ash that coated her tongue. A fading ember spat from the depths of flickering gold-orange flames and hissed as it sank in the snow. Deft fingers forced a blunt iron needle back and forth through coarse green wool and her tears were halted on her cheeks, frozen in icy wind. The fire was dying.

Beyond the blizzard, the shadows of bent trees stood against an endless grey sky, screaming defiance.

She sewed the edges of his cloak. Starting with the collar as he lay unyielding, unmoving and silent as flurries landed and settled in gentle spinning drifts. A flake perched on the end of his nose and she waited for the edges to blur in his breath. Instead it turned to ice and her needle joined the fabric together, pinching it from collar to neck, from chin to nose to forehead. The last flame whispered out of existence. Who would sew her cloak?

~

Fiona Jeeves' Biography

Fiona Jeeves writes fantasy and loves it. Fuelled by coffee, cheese, and stalked by a pair of cats, she is about to publish her debut novel for YA.

She can be found lurking at:
www.fibijeeves.wordpress.com

44: THE MIND, A MINEFIELD OF POSSIBILITIES

by Robert Stewart

Tingling like the aftershock of a shock from some electric storm. My mind was thrashing with feelings north and south the smell of sweet perfume from meadows endless in vast scapes of dreams' succulent warmth.

Vision's limits fully exceeded by zooming vistas on landscape lost in lost control yet focus clear on subject dear soft the touch of imagined warm embrace and lips that kiss the sweetest dew were ever met when my thoughts do turn to you.

A fusion of burning visual moist tender sounds primal to my inner ear and singing to my soul as gripping as a dagger's hand when tender sensual moments that were stolen slow breaths that deepen into caverns as if the rocks, wetted, touch the earth itself.

To fuse a spirit when sharing sounds with words that act as hands and create the perfect interaction with such erythema; much as a breeze with tree tops gently swaying; a union such as this part-thought, part-spirit, part-heart's desire to please. All in a single kiss.

~

Robert Stewart's Biography

No author biography supplied.

45: CAFÉ TERRACE, RUE DU BEURRE, AUTUMN

by Carolyn Cahalane

Whistling waiters drag in shabby red cane chairs. Rain on the ground slishes under car wheels; gun-metal clouds send dancing raindrops to the awning above me, like the scurrying of fairy feet. The brakes of a bus are released in a slow, exasperated gasp.

At the next table, a dark man puts a smooth, rolled cigarette to his craggy mouth. The thick, bitter air fights the garlic and cèpes which long to linger luxuriously. But the rude, mineral-rain air from an open door asserts supremacy, its chill spitefully enveloping my arms.

Entering lugubriously, sliding into seat, a svelte woman in a chartreuse shot-silk dress, hugging her hips like pondweed around a river pebble, flicks her caramel hair pensively, listening to the slow hum of the craggy man's voice, his ochre hands chopping, beckoning, measuring, pointing and, finally, resting on the milky marble table top.

A silver saucer arrives: l'addition.

In the tawdry hotel room, sickly pink walls seep the blabber of American television and I pack, wistfully promising return.

~

Carolyn Cahalane's Biography

Carolyn Cahalane is an English teacher born in Notting Hill, living in South London who is currently writing short stories and a novel set in a school.

46: A SENSE OF FREEDOM

by Alan Pattison

Dennis was never really a religious man, but he always liked going into old churches.

One day, he was walking through a village in Yorkshire when he saw the church, which appeared to be early medieval. The door opened easily and, shortly after walking in, Dennis was greeted by a man in clerical clothes who said, "Please come in and, if you need to know anything, just ask."

Dennis kept walking and looked around him, eventually ending up in the front row of seats. He looked up at the pulpit and admired the fine wood and stonework of the sanctuary. Someone started playing the organ, which always lifted him.

A bit later, through the vestry door, came the smell of cakes being baked and coffee brewed, which made him feel even more relaxed and at home.

Before too long he had the strong sense of being set free and, when he saw the vicar coming towards him, he hailed to ask when the next service would be.

~

Alan Pattison's Biography

No author biography supplied.

47: MORNING

by Diane Caldwell

The taste in her mouth was like metal. Acid. Sour. Her lips were cracked. She ran her tongue over the brittle ridges. She pushed herself up off the bed, grabbed her brown, wool shawl, and flung it around her. Her first steps were painful, like walking on needles. The cold morning air made her skin pucker. She shivered as she prodded along the pinewood boards, wrapping her arms around her chest for warmth, over to the heavy oak door. Pulling it open, her eyes beheld a biblical sunrise. Slants of sunshine radiating out from behind slate clouds like the fingers of God. Golden streaks of light in the gray morning. Doves, "Kerood kerood kerood," and the leaky outside faucet drip drip dripped. She could smell morning. Its misty, dewy-scented freshness. The moist earth. The pine needles rotting.

She made her way back into the house to the kitchen. The pain in her feet had subsided. She put on the kettle. A cup of black coffee would set her straight.

~

Diane Caldwell's Biography

14 years ago, stifling sobs, Diane Caldwell boarded a plane and left the US. Currently she rents a room in Goa, India, where she dances like a banshee at the sunset drum circle, watches sea eagles soar over the jungle, and writes when the muse whispers.

www.adventuresinarambol.blogspot.com

48: GUILTY OF NOTHING

by Bee Grey

I could smell them a distance away. It was that fungus smell. A cross between mouldy and just mildew damp. The smell always seems to permeate down my nose into my mouth; I could taste the smell of fungus. It is not an unpleasant smell or taste, at least not to me.

I headed straight to the mushrooms. They lay slightly hidden behind trees covered with a thick layer of lichen, so soft to the touch. I stepped between the trees, bent down, gently removing the long grass covering the promise of success. A dog barked. Its owner shouted, "What are you doing in there?"

I stood slowly, feeling like a guilty child; not guilty, but feeling guilty just the same. "Collecting mushrooms. Today I think I have found them."

He stood beside me. Looked thoughtfully at my find. Nodded. Taking a knife, he cut through each smooth stalk, carefully placing them in the basket I had brought with me. Breakfast outdoors today?

~

Bee Grey's Biography

No author biography supplied.

49: FEELING A LITTLE SILLY

by John Briscoe

Getting out of bed, Mack sensed the coarseness of the sheets. His mouth tasted like stale sprouts. He picked up his underpants, feeling the stiffness, sniffing the odour. He realised that he'd have to feel his way to the toilet as he could barely see with the curtains closed.

*

Mary heard him get out of bed and, opening her eyes, saw him stagger to the bathroom.

Having seen his body and heard him snore, sniff and thrash about in his sleep all night, she felt relieved nothing had happened between them. Maybe it was the alcohol that had made her fancy him. He'd undressed and, feeling for her, had fallen asleep. She had seen her mistake immediately and heard herself whisper, "What a fool I've been."

She heard Mack shout out; he must have bumped into the lavatory. She should get dressed before he felt a reason to return. If this was a taste of what it would be like, she sensed she would go back to being a nun.

~

John Briscoe's Biography

No author biography supplied.

50: UNDERNEATH

by Emilie Lauren Jones

Shaking arms hugged the splintered remains of the small, wooden mast. Silence. Where would its colossal claws crash through next?

The sweet stench of rotting fruit melded with the scent of dank cellar – another claw raged down on my stolen vessel, throwing me into the frozen depths of the enormous lake. A sickly mix of fear and water flooded my mouth. Gasping, choking, grabbing at something that used to be a part of the base of the boat, I dragged my tired legs on to some floating rubble. Splinters ripped my hands.

Everyone knew not to come here. I should have listened, but the lure of the lonely boat and forbidden mass of inky blackness had proved too tempting. Don't think about what's underneath.

Tears mixed with river slime – would this be my last adventure? If I did escape, no one would believe me anyway – they never did.

~

Emilie Lauren Jones's Biography

Emilie Lauren Jones is a published writer of poetry, short stories and flash fiction. She also runs writing workshops as well as guest speaking. Her poetry collection *Sitting on the Pier* is available to order from Amazon or Waterstones.

www.emilielaurenjones.co.uk

51: KOPI TIAM

by S.W. Hardy

My bloodless knuckles clasp onto the knobbly, off-white plastic stool upon which I sit. The frequent chime of technology constantly reminds me of these distantly-familiar people's dependence upon electricity; multi-coloured screens emit harsh lights and cicada-like moans all around me.

My food arrives on a criss-crossed, blood-red tray.

The aroma of sweaty chicken, ambrosial rice and orientally-fragrant soup hammer at my nostrils. The bird, grain, and liquid were all shades of amber, swirling in the shimmer of oil. It took three minutes 12 seconds to prepare and only cost three dollars. I taste a spoonful of rice, chicken and soup, and my tongue is overloaded with an iridescent rainbow of flavours and textures.

Tender. Herby. Moist. Spicy.

A wayward auburn cockroach scuttles into a cracked drainpipe. I wonder how many other bulbous-eyed, pallid-green lizards were residing in that concrete tube too. My green and gold checkered shirt clings onto my damp skin, as the humid evening air caresses my face.

I decide that I am happy in this land of food.

~

S.W. Hardy's Biography

I graduated from the University of Nottingham with a degree in Creative Writing. I self-published my first Young Adult novel, *No Separation* (available on

Amazon), and run a travel/writing website. I currently live and teach in Shenzhen (China).

www.swhardywriter.com

52: ISLAND

by Jerry Wilson

In the Bahamas, pastels are a sin. Tourists, in heedless pursuit of vacation, spill from leviathan ships in an assault of garish colours, shaming the bleached seagulls into a ghostly chorus of envious screams.

On the pier, a reggae band's insistent, pulsating back-beat sifts through the tourists' sunburned, seasick hangover fog and jerks them into a submissive dance. Popping fingers. Bobbing heads. Swaying hips. Forever changed.

The violent colours of the band's shirts don't merely reflect light, they reach out with kaleidoscopic tentacles and wrench eyeballs from sockets.

In stasis, the white-legged, peacock-hued tourists are obscene. But, animated by the music and inspired by the confident grace of the dancing reggae musicians, they transcend their separate vulgarities and unite in an urgent ritual of ecstasy. They join in a frenzied rapture of whirling indigos, rejoicing crimsons, exulting saffrons, sinuous russets, and graceful ceruleans – bold colours that are proof that they are each part of the celebration.

"I am here, I am alive, I am a part of the shared joy of being."

~

Jerry Wilson's Biography

Being published in Chris Fielden and Allen Ashley's

Sensory Writing Challenge is a step up from writing on the walls of public restroom stalls, right? Wilson is on his way, y'all.

53: SCHOLARS' WALK

by Josie Gowler

We wait in the dark, breath steaming, the bittersweet, slightly metallic taste of our flask of tea lingering on our tongues.

"Ready?" Maude asks in her raspy whisper. Drizzle beads on her hair, picking out the grey in silver baubles. "Coast is clear. Let's go."

Hobbling over a sliding squish of muddy verge we round the corner, stifling giggles, and stop in front of the offensive street sign. 'Scholars Walk'. Really.

Holding onto the icy metal of the sign, I crouch. My knees let out a creak and I feel the cartilage grinding. I take the cap off the marker pen and its heady smell hits me.

One quick stroke later and it's done. 'Scholars' Walk'. Another apostrophe returned. Another city street sign corrected. I nod in satisfaction. So does Maude.

Vandalism to correct vandalism. We rush away, silvered hair flapping in a glacial night-time breeze, tangy with the hint of wood burning in the stoves of the street's affluent houses. We must be England's oldest graffiti artists.

~

Josie Gowler's Biography

Josie Gowler has had short stories published in *365 Tomorrows, Every Day Fiction, Ethereal Tales, Theaker's Quarterly Fiction* and *Perihelion*. Her specialties are weird tales set in the East Anglian Fens and science fiction and fantasy short stories.

54: LOVELY WEATHER FOR DUCKS

by Sandra Unerman

The rain beat against the pavement, pattered among the bare branches of the oak trees in the park and splashed in the stream. Seagulls lined up in a row along the cross bar of the goal down on the playing field and crows flapped overhead. The wind was too strong for an umbrella to be any use. My woolly hat and my big coat kept most of me dry, but I could feel the damp soak into my ankles and cold drops of rain stung my face. The smell of wet grass made my nose itch.

Back home, I looked out into the garden, where puddles and wet rhododendron leaves glittered in a burst of sunshine, before the clouds darkened again. To warm up, I made lemon and ginger tea, with a dash of honey to sweeten the taste.

~

Sandra Unerman's Biography

Sandra Unerman is a writer of fantasy and a member of Clockhouse London Writers. Her novel, *Spellhaven*, is published by Mirror World and she has stories in *Aurora Wolf* online for September 2017 and the anthology, *Fall Into Fantasy* from Cloaked Press.

www.sandraunermanwriter.com

55: THE LIFE OF SARIS

by Dolly Garland

It was the colours that drew me in. Bright, dull, glowing, tacky, iridescent, draped around the shop like glittering wishes, or prophecies. The gorgeous fuchsia for a girls' night out. The boring beige in comfortable cotton when your self-esteem is low. The royal blue to stand out in the crowd, knowing you are better than most. Or a hot fiery red to be a sex-symbol, while the soft chiffon material caresses your skin. The black and silver silk for that fashionable diva who leads, or pure black netted sari for the wannabe-vamp look. The forest green kanjivaram with embroidered flowers to please the mother-in-law, or the shimmering copper that makes your eyes shine and brings the lust-glint back in your husband's eyes. Exquisite emerald for that special dinner party. Tantalising turquoise for a relative's wedding. Dark navy for sombre occasions. The faded yellows and muted pinks for when life is an effort. And white for a widow, offering freedom and independence or grief and endless loneliness.

Take your pick.

What life do you want?

~

Dolly Garland's Biography

Dolly Garland writes stories that are a bit like her – muddled in cultures. She calls London her home, though the roots of her stories have returned to India where

she was born. Find her at:
www.dollygarland.com

56: BAGGAGE

by Laura-Liisa Klaas

I look at my watch for the hundredth time. Surely we should start boarding now for the flight to be on time. The air conditioning is blowing right onto my eyes and cheeks, there is a smell of baked goods mixed with perfume and urine in the air, my palms are sweating on my new chinos and I feel exhausted and fed up. I can still taste the coffee I had two hours ago.

Frowning, I try to look for a mint in my bag. I feel around and almost cry out as my hairbrush prickles the skin underneath my nail. Every time. I should bin the silly thing. I glance down and see a small dot of blood already forming. I sigh and make my way to the toilet to wash it off.

Right when the ice cold water flushes over my throbbing finger, I hear the loud speaker announcing the start of the boarding. I rush out, almost knocking over a toddler. What a great start to my honeymoon, I ponder sarcastically.

~

Laura-Liisa Klaas's Biography

I'm a 30-something Estonian girl living and working in Aberdeen, Scotland and loving it. This year I made myself a promise to start writing my book and therefore I am trying my hand first with the awesome challenges here.

www.schmunny.wordpress.com

57: WANDERING IN WONDERLAND

by Stuart Lanigan

Crackle of the ground underfoot,
Beneath the ice on top,
Hides a hidden underworld,
Causing you to stop.

Listening to the breaking ice,
Stepping in and stamping twice,
Watching as the ice shards shatter,
Laughing aloud like it doesn't matter.

The ice cold air is freezing,
Breathing out in clouds of steam,
Wandering in wonderland,
In a bitter winter scene...

~

Stuart Lanigan's Biography

I'm 60, upright and alive, working hard, just trying to survive.

58: THE DENTIST

by Karen McDermott

I closed my eyes against the too-white ceiling, the inquisitive flare of the dentist's nostrils, and opened my ears instead to the radio's distraction.

The cliché of soothing classical music had been vetoed by the young practitioner, who seemed to have a preference for bubblegum pop. I focussed on her soft humming along to some pipsqueak belittling her ex, before the sterile smell of her gloves pushing my top lip into a snarl jerked me back to reality. My heartbeat quickened as I heard the assistant shuffling away to select another instrument of terror.

"You're just going to feel a little prick," the voice above me assured.

"Mhmmpf," I replied, attempting to keep the fug of panic escaping my throat and clouding all of our judgements.

Friends had had plenty to say about the process, but curiously left out the sound of old boughs breaking. The deforestation of my mouth leaving a few birches standing still.

A receptionist handed me my bill, and I wondered at my pristinely uniformed lumberjack, who'd pulped my wallet too.

~

Karen McDermott's Biography

Karen is an NHS amanuensis and writer of listings for

What's On magazine in Brighton. She likes going to gigs, reading books she finds left on windowsills in the street, energy drinks, and not going to the dentist.

Find Karen on Twitter: @Karen_S_McD

59: A BAD COFFIN FIT

by George Kelly

When he awoke, he saw nothing but black.

He tried to lift his head, but it bumped against a hard surface. His bare elbows grazed against rough wood. His feet scraped the end of the box.

Above ground, he heard voices; then, louder, sprinkles of mud and gravel raining on top of his new house. To make it worse, the space smelled of wet socks: musty, tickling his nostrils.

He wished Leena, his wife, was here to hold him close, to kiss the salty tears leaking down his cheeks. He wished he hadn't crossed Mario Sorelli.

He waited.

Then, loud as a truck, a series of gunshots shattered his thoughts – followed by two heavy thumps from above, bodies falling to ground.

Minutes later, the coffin was opened and light flooded the small space, momentarily blinding him.

When he could see again, his wife smiled back at him.

"I knew you'd find me," he said, and, after she helped him out, he kissed her.

"I love you," she said.

"I love you too," he said.

The last thing he remembered about that day was the taste of her lips: strawberry lip-butter with a hint of blood.

~

George Kelly's Biography

George is currently signed to literary agent Piers Blofeld, and is in the process of preparing his latest novel, *One Knife Stand,* for traditional publication. He's had short stories published all around the world. You can find him at:

www.georgekellyfiction.com

60: A FISHY TALE

by John Notley

Each step he took towards the chippy excited him as the unmistakable aroma of the delights to come wafted from the open doorway and assailed his nostrils. As he entered he heard the plop as a fresh fillet of fish fell into the fat fryer and the frizzling sound was music to his ears. The pan of boiling oil sizzled in harmony with it.

He placed his order for cod and chips and took his seat in anticipation of the joy to follow. When his order arrived he was tempted to test the texture before tasting. With his index finger he prodded the recumbent fish and, satisfied, picked up the sauce bottle.

The tart taste of the tartare sauce, which he spread liberally over the dish, added to the succulent sensation as it encountered his palate. He savoured every mouthful as if it were his last meal. This was a moment never to be forgotten. Working abroad had been lucrative, but they couldn't cook fish and chips. Good to be home again.

~

John Notley's Biography

John, a retired travel agent, having failed to make his fortune has taken up his pen again, hoping to redress the situation. He had a few stories and poems published some years ago but feels it's time to hit the jackpot.

www.linkedin.com/in/john-notley-503666102/

61: RELEASE

by Temmy Oj

The water was her release...

...and as tears rolled down her cheeks, the salty tasting liquid intermingling with the sharp, chlorine-scented water, bubbles rose to the surface of the disturbed liquid. She imagined she was one of them; free to turn her dreams into reality, free to fly. Her hair flew wildly in the water, circling her head like a halo. Her bare feet stung as they pushed up to the surface, but her clothes weighed her down. It was almost surreal.

Almost.

She felt its soft, fluid movements dance along with her. Its motherly touch guided her. The water's receptive energy allowed her to empty her mind and to free herself of the thoughts that burdened her. The water extinguished the flames of pain and anguish that roared within her. The dulled sounds removed her from reality, the cool liquidity protected her from the stones life threw at her. It encased her in an impenetrable shell of self-importance. For once it was just about her.

She was the water.

The water was her.

~

Temmy Oj's Biography

I am a 15 year old writer, who enjoys writing flash fiction. I also like listening to slam poetry when I have time and also attempting to write some. You can read some of my pieces on my blog:

www.temmyoblog.wordpress.com

62: EXIT WOUND

by Wayne Hewitt

Strewn naked and face down on the mortician's table, the cadaver captivated my gaze, synapses exploding. I struggled to comprehend what I was seeing. Feeling my eyes drying to the point of pain, I forced myself to blink, applying much needed lubrication. *That's a dead body*, I thought. *Whoa. This was going to be the weirdest first day at a new job.*

The exit wound gave a clue to the cause of death, but never assume anything, my university professor had said. I placed my right ear over the exit wound. There was a faint whoosh, like when you listen to a shell at the seaside. Hmm... I wonder... no one else is here. Why not?

My gloveless right index finger eased into the exit wound. It felt pleasantly squishy, almost erotic. I heaved in a deep smell of my gore covered finger, salivating at the fragrance of death. Oh boy, placing the finger in my mouth I savoured the taste of my first client's soul.

I think I'm going to enjoy being a mortician.

~

Wayne Hewitt's Biography

Australia is now home for this proud son of Yorkshire. An adventurous spirit has seen me travel the world working, experiencing, laughing and crying, but mostly enjoying as many shenanigans as I could get involved in... Let the adventures continue.

63: SCARED OF...?

by Abhi Shan

A pair of gentle footsteps broke the chain of my thoughts. I realised that I had been staring at the roof for a while.

Martha was there with a cup of brewed coffee. I could feel the tug of magic beans as aroma filled my nostrils and my stomach growled.

"Have you overcome your fear of food?" she asked.

Remembering the events from last evening – headache, disorientation, and episodes of vomiting among many other things – brought a bit of burning bile juice to my throat.

"I'm not afraid of food. I'm scared of putting it in my mouth," I replied.

"So you aren't going to eat anything?" she asked.

"I'm not sure," I said.

She came forward with a piece of lemon cake on a plate. My stomach rumbled and a sudden gush of saliva filled my mouth, making me unable to speak without spitting.

"I guess your thoughts are scarier than anything in the fridge," she said when I was busy gobbling down the cake.

I smiled sheepishly.

~

Abhi Shan's Biography

Abhi Shan is a research scientist by profession and an

avid reader. When he is not busy doing science, he loves to write short stories and flash fictions.

64: MURDER BY THE POND

by James Moore

The hot green algae covered pond was slightly shaded by the sycamores, cottonwoods and the one water maple at its edge. My dog, Sugar, lay a couple feet away in the shade of a cedar. Its berries would waft a juniper scent in the humid Southern summer-air.

The pond had an acrid air about it, from the cows urinating while they drank. My eyes scanned the still waters looking for cottonmouths or turtles. Momma hates turtles. They eat her fish.

The dog's ear twitched. She cocked her head. The bark on the cedar tree erupted in scratching. I span. I shot. I didn't see. A dead squirrel fell to the rock I was sitting on. BB through the head. I was in shock. I pulled the trigger and didn't see. Sugar jumped up and snatched it away triumphantly. She'd got a meal.

I was looking for turtles and snakes.

I shouldn't have shot that squirrel.

~

James Moore's Biography

James Moore grew up farming in rural Tennessee. As a child he studied nature and read a lot since there was no cable television or internet. Now, an engineer, he enjoys writing his observations and telling stories.

65: PURPLE

by Paul Phillips

As, with the lightest of touches – a robin on a fork handle – I press down upon the cool, chrome lever, my half-hearted knock still sounding in my ears, I taste the sharp flavour of the molecules of methyl ester, pick up the pineapple odour of the perfume, and know before even catching a glimpse of the consulting room that it's going to be a woman.

Blushing, heart pounding, I enter. She gestures towards the chair with a waft of Nivea and hand sanitiser. Greasy stains, seemingly a mixture of soot and surgical iodine, have overwhelmed the worn shellac of the uninviting arm rests and penetrated the grain. I ease myself onto the flaking vinyl cushion with a furfuraceous squeak that conjures up the texture of shell middens – a racial memory – or at the very least, the poor quality leather of an early Mazda MX5.

"What seems to be the trouble?" Her voice shimmers like a stained-glass bead-curtain.

"It's my..." I can only mouth the word. "Should it really be that colour?"

~

Paul Phillips' Biography

Paul Phillips writes short and long fiction across a variety of genres. He lives in Derbyshire with several humans and a hairy brown thing.

www.bypaulphillips.com

66: THE DROP

by Ben Clarke

The sting in my eyes from sweat reminded me of the burn from raw onions. I was unable to wipe it away due to the large helmet over my head. Removing it, even to stop the sweat which was running down my face like a trickling tap, was a felony during a combat drop.

I tried to focus on something else, tried to keep my balance without holding on to the support rail as we bounced through the sky at breakneck speed. Soon the dull drone of the gunship's engines, like air conditioning on full power, was replaced by a new sound. It was like closing your eyes on November 5th and feeling explosions with bass-riddled booms radiating into your bones. These weren't fireworks though.

A feeling of anxiety filled my stomach. We were descending rapidly. The radio crackled in my ear.

"30 seconds, standby."

The explosions were loud. With each one the craft shook. My only distraction was the sting in my eyes.

Then the doors opened.

"Go, go, go."

~

Ben Clarke's Biography

I'm from Norfolk, UK. I enjoy writing for fun only, love Sci-Fi, war and general action genres. Married father of 4 and Ambulance EMT.

67: LAUNCH

by Mab Jones

The astronauts are strapped into their seats and countdown has begun. Mission control is a lone male voice, but booming, echoing, ricocheting across me, hammering into my eardrums. I can taste the sound as it pierces, bullet-quick, into my soft body as I wait at the side of the launch site.

The astronauts are excited but, here, the situation is having the opposite effect, my adrenals gunning, brain fizzing, stomach pulsing like a sick animal in the hot sack of my body. All I can taste is sweat and smoke; all I can see is a multicolour blur, buzzing beyond rainbow into nightmarish white light.

Minutes explode, a cosmos of sound and fury, and I feel like a planet collapsing in on itself; but, eventually, the rocket has returned, and my son, the astronaut, is running my way.

"That was fun," he screeches, comet-ing into me as I wobble. "Can I go again?"

"Mummy just needs a sit-down, first," I say, and the astronaut, the little boy, transforms into an ambulance and begins to wail.

~

Mab Jones's Biography

Mab Jones is an award-winning poet and writer from Wales. She has authored two poetry collections, presents programmes on BBC Radio 4, teaches at

Cardiff University, and runs International Dylan Thomas Day.

Find Mab on Twitter: @mabjones

68: INDIGO

by Frances Hay

Jordan thinks Isaac Newton was a cheat. Try as hard as he can, Jordan only sees six colours in the rainbow. He tells Sara, that mantra ROYGBIV, it's such a scam, allowing yourself two separate blues.

Jordan doesn't believe in indigo.

But indigo haunts Sara's family. Her grandma told her about the indigo fields of the Low Country, the rough touch of her own grandfather's stained fingers, still deep blue, long after he was freed.

These days, in the High Country, in their cabin surrounded by bare, tan hills as sculpted as a bodybuilder's arms, Jordan never looks at the sky. He stares at pages of the internet, searching for physics jobs.

Sara lifts the heavy stoneware dish from the lemon-scented suds onto the wooden rack, wiping her hands on her apron. Outside the window, the afternoon mists break into an arch of fractured light. For the first time ever, she sees what Newton saw, what Jordan will never see. Between the pale blue and the violet, there pulses a deeper, sadder blue.

~

Frances Hay's Biography

Frances Hay is an American writer living in Wales. Her short fiction has appeared in *damselfly press, Persimmon Tree* and Café Aphra. Her novel *The Night*

Fogs will be published in 2018 by Holland House Books.

69: THE DRAUGHTSMAN

by Tina Smith

Thick smoke stung my throat as I entered the room. Everyone looked up and stared. A gaunt man with a cigarette hanging out the side of his mouth croaked, “Hello darling. Want a drink?” The inch of ash clinging to the end of his cigarette gave up, falling onto a drawing on the table in front of him.

He pointed at a percolator bubbling away on a Formica table next to a blueprinting machine which stank of ammonia. I nodded, apologising to a man who stood up just as I squeezed past. He smelt of sour cream and whiskey. My cheek left damp from its brief brush with his chest.

I poured myself a coffee as thick as a good gravy. It tasted metallic, the caffeine hitting my brain with startling velocity. In every direction beaming topless women, with drawing pins through their foreheads, stared back at me over the days of July 1986. I was the only woman without a pin.

I nervously sat at a spare drawing board and adjusted the parallelogram machine.

~

Tina Smith’s Biography

Tina is currently working on her first fantasy novel. She also writes short stories and film scripts. In 2014 she won ‘Best Horror’ at the Limelight Film Awards and an award at the British Horror Film Festival.

70: A SENSE OF PLACE

by Sara Roberts

Ernest leant in the doorway.

The people were beautiful and clean and stood laughing and drinking cocktails from jars. The men had long hair and small beards and open-necked shirts. The women had short hair and earrings and kaftans. The incense smelled expensive.

He felt hungry but it was a different kind of hunger, and he knew he wouldn't find what he needed here.

The next morning was hot and the sun beat down like lead. By the time he reached the place on the other side of town, sweat ran down him in small rivers, prickling his skin.

A woman with hard eyes and long nails stood counting money by the bar. In the corner, two men played pool in silence. The balls ricocheted loudly around the table. The ceiling fan turned, stirring the air. The counter was sticky with hundreds of nights of drinking. He could taste the smoke, gritty in the back of his throat.

Yes, this was what he'd been looking for.

This was where he would set his novel.

~

Sara Roberts' Biography

Sara Roberts discovered flash fiction in 2011. She has been shortlisted for the Fish Publishing prize and her work has appeared in *Ink in Thirds, From the Depths* and

Corvus Review. She also runs Café Aphra, an online writing community.

www.cafeaphrapilot.blogspot.co.uk

71: TWO PINK LINES

by Sarah Peloquin

Her sight was the first thing to go wonky. Everything looked brighter and the limited colour spectrum seen by humans expanded by hues. She'd never seen the Midwest in technicolour before, but Kansas had just transformed into the wonderful land of Oz.

Taste hit her next. Flavours burst on her tongue in an overwhelming explosion. And by explosion, she meant Armageddon style. Food she would usually eat a few days after its expiration had the awful tang of too-ripe. Gagging became a normal side-effect of opening her refrigerator door. She could devour an entire jar of dill pickles, but her favourite apple had her heading for the porcelain goddess, where she quickly discovered smell was the next sense to go.

It was definitely time to clean the toilet. And don't get her started on the newly-showered children who still smelled like a cow pasture. Her husband's kisses might have been minty-fresh, but the toothpaste did nothing to cover the fact that the human mouth is a disgusting place.

The positive sign just confirmed her suspicions.

~

Sarah Peloquin's Biography

Sarah Peloquin loves being the wife of her own knight in shining, but slightly dented, armour. Together they created three beautiful children – a princess, and two little princes. Sarah writes of life and love in the midst of her adventures.

www.srhplqn.wordpress.com

72: ALIVE

by Abigail Williamson

Boom.

A wave crashed over his head, sucking him downwards. Exhaustion beat a path through his pulsating veins, quietening them into submission. Lungs on fire, throat parched, his head throbbed. Strange to be in the water and yet feel so dry. Salt will do that. His skin shrieked pain; macerated and wrinkled beyond recognition.

"Help." The words stuck.

Whoosh.

He was under. Deeper into some sort of black, tight space. Arms and legs stuck to his aching body. Suffocating now. No air. Unable to fight, he squeezed his eyes shut.

Darkness closed in.

"Am I dead?"

Silent speech hurts the brain.

Crack.

He jolted awake.

Bright lights. Strange faces. Hands grabbing. Loud voices. Feet running. Cold steel.

"Am I in hell?"

He cried out. At long last.

She was feeding him. Something warm, sticky sweet.

He knew her. He did. He studied her face intently. Lips soft and pink. Smiling. Eyes warm and tender. Something familiar in her voice.

She held him close.

"Welcome to the world, little Harry," she soothed.

"Mama." He smiled back.

~

Abigail Williamson's Biography

No author biography supplied.

73: WIND AND SPEED

by Tim Baker

Stationary, engine idling, power itching to be released. Gently release the clutch while equally gently twisting the accelerator and we're off. Even at walking pace the gyroscopic forces generated by the whirling gears keep it stable.

Up to 20 everything is calm: engine purring, like a leopard prowling the savannah looking for prey. Sleek, composed, ready for action. Faster, you feel the breeze. 30 is fine, especially if the weather is warm.

40, eyes water if you've no cover. Tears pushed along the side of your head. Feel the wind on your body, bank the bike for tighter bends. 50 and the wind whistles past your ears. 60, relax and lean into it, like a cushion under your chest. Engine vibration, noise and wind mingle. 70, don't grip too tight to the thin handlebars, lean lower. Thick leather jacket contoured onto your body like a wet linen shirt. Wind roars as the helmet presses into your forehead, only the strap prevents it being ripped off.

You and the machine are one, thirsty for more.

~

Tim Baker's Biography

Tim is a market researcher, a rower and is trying to be a writer. He's been saying for as long as he can remember that next year he'll be a rower, a writer and occasional market researcher. Hope springs eternal.

74: THE HUNTRESS

by Maddy Hamley

The tall grass tickled Cleo's nose as she basked in glorious sunshine. The smell of warm, crumbly earth, with a hint of the freshly-mown lawn from next door, wafted over the garden. She closed her eyes, relishing the peace.

A loud rustle, a *thump*. Cleo opened her eyes and saw the long, green blades jerk suddenly just a few metres away.

She rose silently, tensing her powerful muscles as she crept towards the swishing grass. A black-plumed bird was hacking at the ground, throwing up clouds of dry dirt in its frenzy.

The perfect prey.

She watched intently, poised to strike, already imagining the taste of hot blood and dark meat on her tongue.

"Kitty."

Cleo jumped at the deafening outburst. The bird squawked in alarm as it took off in a flurry of feathers.

Irate, Cleo glared at the source of the noise as it approached with dull, plodding thumps, grinning down at her obliviously from a grubby, tanned face.

"There you are, kitty."

~

Maddy Hamley's Biography

Maddy Hamley is a bilingual English-German translator

and full-time project manager. When she's not busy cursing at untranslatable Bavarian proverbs, she enjoys writing short stories, singing, or lounging around in Cologne with her fiancée.

www.madham.org

75: ON A DATE AT THE MOVIES (OR, A TOE-CURLING CASE OF STARRY-EYED NOSTALGIA)

by Amanda Garzia

"Imagine if we'd been there," he whispered, his waxed beard tickling her neck as the closing credits rolled to the shrill trumpet notes of the jaunty score.

She paused, Parmesan-tipped fingers flat over her salty lips, cheeks bulging with the last palmful of fluffy flakes of popcorn.

"Drinking emerald-coloured absinthe," he went on, "tapping to ragtime, rubbing shoulders with Paris's avant-garde and its fiery genius."

She sank deeper in the plush poppy armchair, admiring the cloud-specked sky of the ceiling mural. "Or feasting on Champagne and plump strawberries, leafing through Proust to the murmur of the Seine."

"The Belle Époque."

"It had its moments of lustre."

"Would that we have lived then, happily ever after."

"Our bliss wouldn't have lasted."

"I thought you loved me."

"Precisely."

"Do clarify."

"Paris would soon be deserted, its men sent to the front where they would squelch in filthy trenches, bodies crawling with lice, shell-shocked, risking capture, disfigurement, and death. Need I go on? With the Great War on our doorstep we'd have been cruelly, if not forever, parted."

~

Amanda Garzia's Biography

At age 12, Amanda typed the first edition of her own (now defunct) magazine, posting copies to Canadian friends left behind on coming to Malta. Having written for *The Times of Malta*, *Pink,* and *Child*, she's presently concentrating on fiction.

www.facebook.com/mandy.garzia

76: JUST TO FEEL SOMETHING

by M M Lewis

I wanted to feel something, anything.

The odd individual who sold me the pill laughed. “You’ll feel everything,” he said.

I put the pill in my mouth. It was dry and harsh on my tongue; no sweetener. It melted. It was like opening my eyes for the first time. Like an artist had painted washes over the surroundings.

The usual brown sea at Weston, now a vibrant Aegean blue. The usual bland smell was now a banquet of aromas: seaweed, succulent fish, even a whiff of exotic flowers from far away. I followed my nose. It was a memorial bouquet of yellow roses, up on the rocks. I had to get a closer sniff.

I climbed up. The surface was unbearably sharp, but the scent drove me on. I gritted my teeth and stretched: just out of reach – I lost footing and fell, far below. The extreme amplification extended to the sensation of pain. Stabs of agony attended every attempt at movement. I could feel everything.

~

M M Lewis’s Biography

M M Lewis is widely published in the independent press, including the *British Fantasy Society Journal*, *Theaker’s Quarterly* and *Wordland.* He lives by the sea in the South West of England. For more of his work check out his blog:

www.syntheticscribe.wordpress.com

77: BLOOMING MARVELLOUS

by Christine O'Donnell

Her first thought was of roses – red as death and dripping in the perfume of their own importance. Opening her eyes, the velvet darkness was calming somehow. She felt peace, as she breathed in the overwhelming scent of her second life.

She felt the wooden veneer shatter under the strength of her new nails, as she burrowed rapidly through her temporary home. Her hands touched soil, squeezing it between her icy palms until it squelched.

She surveyed the town she had just left the week before, magnificent somehow now that she could taste the metallic joy of her next meal.

She tested her heightened senses – the feel of trees caressing her cheeks, smells of greasy chicken miles away, the sound of someone swallowing while drinking.

Then a new sensation. Footsteps. A rapid heartbeat. A wooden stake. A final taste of her disintegrating ash. Dead again. Blooming marvellous.

~

Christine O'Donnell's Biography

Christine is an English teacher by day and writing sleuth by night, with numerous sojourns into the fanciful in her work. She has recently published her first teen historical fiction on Amazon and continues to dream of one day making it big, or even small.

78: OLD SPICES

by Namita Mukherjee

In ancient times in India, guests were worshipped like gods. As soon as they appeared in the house they were provided cold water: to drink and wash their feet.

The dinner was served with enormous items of food to please the five senses.

Usually, on a thali: bitter curry with rice was given to start, which was cooked with Nim or Korola, to increase the guests' appetite.

Salt was essential for any cooking and it made a meal enjoyable and unrefined salt was better for health.

Salt and chillies had been used together to cook the tasty curries for guests; chillies contain up to seven times more vitamin C, A and E. It also helped to relieve migraine, muscle, joint and nerve pains.

Sour dishes were prepared with green mangoes and tamarind which had major health benefits. Finally, the sweet dishes were presented to the honourable guests and they returned their blessing or well wishes to their hosts.

I presume, in those days, nobody knew about vitamins; the wellbeingness around food had come orally.

~

Namita Mukherjee's Biography

I have been writing since I was seven years old, but those writings were in the Bengali language. I've always enjoyed writing, especially short stories which are on women's emancipation. After finishing a short story writing course I have more confidence writing in English.

79: BY THE SEA

by Sandy Phillips

The screech of seagulls came soaring and swooping, just past my ear this sunny day. I felt the whoosh of wings on salty air sail by, making me jump. Their feathers were ragged and barely white.

The tips of their flight feathers raised them on the current of soft balmy air after snatching my bag of tangy vinegar chips. They flew high, followed by others all trying to pinch my lunch.

The brown paper bag fell to earth, followed by squabbling shrieks and sharp pecks, along with grasping claws all aimed at the contents. Beady eyes dared the others to take a dainty morsel. The whole bunch merged into a crazy turmoil – a noisy, flapping heap.

The crushed oily container was whipped away by a cold gust that blew up. Gradually, one by one, replete birds untangled themselves and flew off, leaving a greasy grey stain.

~

Sandy Phillips' Biography

My book, *The Narrow Doorway*, about psychic activities, is available on Amazon. I write articles and have poems in many anthologies.

I belong to the Enfield Poets and attend sessions with Allen Ashley. I especially enjoyed reading poetry to jazz.

80: MESSAGE IN A BOTTLE

by Lizzie Merrill

The brilliant sun blazed in the cloudless sapphire sky. Jan strolled barefoot along the seashore, the soft golden sand tickling her toes. The distinctive smell of the ocean teased her nostrils. Fishy, with a slightly sulphurous but also briny tang. The waves broke gently on the beach; jagged rocks were revealed by the ebb tide.

Jan caught a glimpse, a flash of reflected sunlight, in her peripheral vision. What was that? She beelined to inspect the mystery object; a jade-green bottle. Clasping it by the neck and caressing the cool, smooth glass, she realised there was something inside. Looking closely, she detected a rolled up sheet of paper. Jan examined the yellow cork and worked it loose. She heard a loud pop as it left the bottle. Intrigued, Jan slid the paper out. It slowly unrolled. Peering at the squiggly writing, she deciphered the message:

We are pleased to announce:
Allen's Sensory Overload Challenge.
Tell a story in under 175 words.
Use copious sensory description.

Jan beamed. "Challenge accepted."

~

Lizzie Merrill's Biography

Lizzie Merrill lives near Chesterfield, Derbyshire. After many years as a stay-at-home mum, she now works as a part-time library assistant. Her current project is a historical romance, *Letters from Esther*.

www.lizziemerrill.com

81: SLUGS

by Jayne Buckland

Extra strong slugs began slithering through the cat flap. The little muscly brown and grey ridged bodies, smothered in gloopy gel, with frilly flesh orange skirts and antennae repulsed my senses.

I would catch the ugly sight of them, up to five hanging like a hand of crooked, fat fingers over the edges of my china cat-feeding bowls. They could not resist the pungent smell of fishy flaked salmon leftovers, smelling high, like seaweed baked in the sun.

One tried sliding behind my skirting board. I grabbed its tail. That body can stretch multiple times. It felt like a large, over ripe, stoneless Spanish olive, in oil.

I set a trap with fish flavoured cat biscuits in the garden. They slid out and mouths engaged in frenzied sucking noises all night long. Dawn came up. “The enemy of my enemy is my friend.” Magpies lined up on the roof, swooped down and picked the slugs off.

~

Jayne Buckland’s Biography

No author biography supplied.

82: NOSING AROUND

by Lynn-Marie Harper

When her cold disappeared she found she was left with a sense of smell that she didn't recognise as her own. The city she was in wafted extremely as she passed by a putrid drain being repaired. The gelateria by the beach indicated that ice-cream did smell, she just hadn't known. She too smelt in the 34° of heat. Had she known, she would have included a deodorant in the liquids bag.

The meat in the charcuteria was a multitude of aromas, as was the sweet-smelling pasteleria next door. The hotel lobby's vibrant cleanliness amazed her and even the air-conditioner wafted warm, croissant-like. Almonds from the bag roasted deliciously anew as she chewed them. Coffee's bitterness complemented the fragrances emitting from the perfume shops and pharmacies. The mustiness of the cathedral's crypt was as pungent as the sea's ozone freshness.

She'd read a book about smell once. She'd nose it out when she got back and sniff her way to the place that it reposed.

~

Lynn-Marie Harper's Biography

Lynn-Marie writes mainly poetry, with sorties into life writing and fiction, and has been published in print and online publications. She lives in London and has most recently worked in libraries and read to hospice patients

for several years.
www.miralinka1.wordpress.com

83: FLASHBACKS

by Faye Minton

Hand visibly shaking and bittersweet, salty tears glistening in my eyes, I lift the crisp, yellowed photograph from the suffocatingly dusty trunk into my hand. The Eiffel Tower. With him – my soft-skinned, homely smelling fiancé. Memories flood back, and I feel a smile tease my trembling lips.

The immaculate shot was taken at around two on the afternoon of a welcomingly warm June day. With our bellies satisfied by greasy, crunchy, fried bread and sweet tea, we had gazed up at the towering structure, beaming. All around us, bright, flashing cameras were clicking, children were laughing with their high pitched, innocent giggles and birds were singing, calling to their friends. None of this could be seen in the image, of course, but just a glance of it violently threw me into the flashbacks, unprepared and unprotected. But I didn't mind, not really...

~

Faye Minton's Biography

No author biography supplied.

84: PINK, PECULIAR, PERFECT

by Etheray

I sniffed at the air. I couldn't fathom why, but the first thing that came to my mind was jasmines.

"Can I take it off now?" I mumbled. No reply. I stripped the highly inappropriate, neon pink blindfold off anyway.

"Happy April Fools." A bouquet of tulips – that strangely reeked of jasmines – blurred my vision momentarily as it flew past like a demented bird and landed with a thump in the stinking basin. The next thing I saw was Fabian's triumphant grin. "And HAPPY BIRTHDAY."

"What?" I asked.

It was only then that I glanced around me. Wow. What better place to receive a bouquet of flowers, from your best buddy, than the *lavatory*.

He tapped on his phone a few times, and out blasted a recording of him singing the happy birthday song, way off-key. To Fabian, birthdays are for fooling around, for doing nonsensical stuff.

"Open wide," I ordered. I popped a strawberry-flavoured sweet into Fabian's mouth, as thanks. It was pink. His favourite.

"Yum." He grinned widely. "Ready for an awesome day?"

~

Etheray's Biography

Etheray is a 15-year-old girl who loves the colourful world of writing because she loves expression. She believes she can become an author someday – and with that belief she practises writing on her blog. Follow and support her at:

www.mydream-journey-destination.blogspot.my

85: FEARLESS

by Elizabeth McGinty

"Did you see something move across the garden?" I ask my husband as he peers at the TV screen.

"What?" he asks.

"I'm sure I saw a movement across the patio, I hope it's not a mouse." No response.

I venture into the garden, treading cautiously. I dislike mice. Their fast, furry bodies and long tails make me feel nauseous. I relax, as I inhale the smell of honeysuckle, and almost forget my purpose.

I bend to pick up the overturned watering can and an icy chill runs down my spine as something moves inside it. I'm rooted to the spot, adrenaline courses through my body. Fight or flight.

I peek over the rim, ready to drop and run. Two large eyes blink back at me from a gorgeous dark-green body. Not a mouse, but a frog. For a moment, I contemplate placing my lips against his smooth damp skin. Well a girl can hope... Instead, I carry him to the edge of the solar fountain, and set him free.

~

Elizabeth McGinty's Biography

Elizabeth McGinty is a short story writer. She has been published by *The People's Friend*, and has self-published a novella *The Secret of the Vineyard*, under the pen name, Georgie Faye.

Find Elizabeth on Twitter: @Pen_Paper_Write

86: HOLIDAY

by Ros Byrne

The aptly-named footwear flip-flopped gently against my soles. The sea breeze was the temperature of a hairdryer. As the beach seared my now bare feet, I hot-footed it into the cold shallows of the Atlantic. Relief. Blistered toes relishing the gritty sand, I paddled along, parallel to the shimmering horizon.

"Daddy, Daddy."

My small daughter, spade aloft, came running. I swooped her up, her brimming bucket spilling over me. Wet sandy legs wound instinctively round my back. I kissed her salty face, nuzzling her tangled blonde hair which smelt of lemon shampoo and sunshine.

"I caught a crab. Look, look." We knelt to peer in the yellow pail.

"Mmm. Supper?" I teased.

Squealing in horror, she skipped off back to her brothers in the rock pools, swinging the crab in his briny jail. Her mother called me from the shady beach bar and minutes later ice-cold beers were working their magic. From behind the shack, a pungent aroma of sardines and peppers charring on the barbecue wafted over. Irresistible. Perhaps the prisoner would go free.

~

Ros Byrne's Biography

No author biography supplied.

87: THE PERFUMED GARDENER

by Louis Cennamo

Capability smelt a rat; a scent overpoweringly malodourous, even for a metaphor.

"Time to sniff out this pungent weed and uproot it," he exclaimed. A whiff of an idea ping-ed through the pong, back and forth, wafting in waves of whiff-whaffs.

"Orchids, roses... my most beautiful thoughts."

He began to plant their seeds in the fertile soil of his fervent imagination, certain that the flagrantly fragrant ethereal essences would inspire him to a sixth sense, subtly betwixt scents.

His mind got to work, to factor in a factory of olfactory factuals – such charismatic aromatics, to scintillate... illuminate... exhilarate. But first...

"To FUMIGATE. Take the plunge... expunge... the grunge."

He sniffled a snuff, snuffled a sniff. How long had this rodent been buried in the darkest recesses of his unconscious undersoil, or even its subconscious subsoil?

His snout dug deep, the stench soon threw in the towel to his snouty trowel. "EU-REEK-AH." His blast, heaven's scent at last.

"As the seed – so the trees, and flowers in my perfumed garden, I will come out of this smelling of roses."

~

Louis Cennamo's Biography

Louis Cennamo is a much travelled pro musician, holistic healer and creative writer, currently working on a collection of his 'quirky' metaphysical short stories, 10 of which have been published at time of writing, in online magazines and printed anthologies.

88: RIGHT OUT OF THE SCREEN AT YOU

by Jonathan Macho

I'm excited. Smello-hearo-toucho-tasteo-seeo-telo-vision. (Aren't the last three the same thing? Eh.) Hot off the presses, fresh off the shelves, mint in box. This changes everything. It is no exaggeration to say that civilisation, nay, the whole human paradigm will be forever changed once these are in every home. And I have the first. I am a pioneer. Like Louis Armstrong off the moon, except on my sofa.

I plug in, pick up the remote and hit 'ON'.

My god.

The smell of Albert Square hits me like a bin lorry. I sniff, and get something between endless, cyclical despair and a chip shop curry. *MasterChef* is on next, and I take the main right off of Greg Wallace's plate. It tastes incredible, like... real food, or something. I can hear him cursing so distinctly.

I change the channel, reach out, and caress the flames bursting from a dragon's mouth. I pull away before he has my arm off. The third degree burns feel so real. The smell of charred flesh fills my living room.

Incredible.

~

Jonathan Macho's Biography

Jonathan Macho is a recently-ish graduated student, lost in the big wide world, with a passion for writing and a frenzied imagination. He lives in Cardiff with his family and a talking space raccoon who definitely exists.

89: SWEATING YOUR ONIONS

by Patricia Mudge

A pungent smell of onions caramelising on the griddle alongside succulent, meaty sausages wafted into Tom's nostrils, telling his brain he was starving.

He ordered a large hotdog with onions from a guy with clammy hands and beads of sweat dripping from his brow. Tom watched wide-eyed as a droplet slithered down his nose and hung precariously on the end. Gravity was doing its best to pull that bubble down – it was a bottom-heavy teardrop – when to Tom's relief, the guy finally wiped the sweat away with his sleeve.

Ignoring the grossness with hotdog in hand, Tom salivated in anticipation as he topped it with a dollop of ketchup and mustard. He chomped down hard.

"Hmmm." His taste buds tingled, as the heady mix hit his tongue, and his chin, his shirt, his trousers and his new trainers.

Chuckling, the sweaty hotdog guy said, "Ugh, gross."

~

Patricia Mudge's Biography

I entered university as a mature student and completed my first degree followed by the PGCE in primary teaching. Since retiring, I've self-published a children's picture book, *Mrs Merryweather's Magic Fingers,* and I've written longer stories for older children.

90: ENTERTAINMENT THIS EVENING

by Ejder S. Raif

Ronald was woken by a sound like cats screeching. He peered out of his bedroom window to see a group of people arguing with a glamorous-looking woman. Ronald screwed up his face as her perfume filled the air.

"You are so inconsiderate," said one woman. "Talking on your phone at the top of your voice. People are trying to sleep."

"And I'm trying to sort out a very important problem," replied the glamorous-looking woman.

"Show some respect," said one man.

Ronald couldn't take his eyes off this glamorous-looking woman. However, he soon turned away, as staring too hard would make his eyes pop out.

As he closed his window to go back to bed, he was relieved that the arguments had finally ended.

Suddenly, the room felt cold. He placed his hand on the radiator. It was as cold as ice. He switched it on to warm it up.

Then he went downstairs to make a hot drink. As he drank it, it was like ashes in his mouth.

~

Ejder S. Raif's Biography

Ejder S. Raif has been published in Issue 2 of *Boscombe Revolution* and in NUHA Foundation's 2013 *Blogging Prizes*. He lives in London and works as a Support Worker, as well as an Assistant Communications Officer.

91: THE WORLD AS IT SHOULD BE

by Charley Swire

Wicked winds whipped soft skin, forcing pale faces to flush red. The setting sun turning the sky into a beautiful canvas carelessly streaked with reds, pinks and oranges. The smell of dead leaves was overpowering, but not entirely unpleasant as each crunched underfoot.

Individual sounds from the treetop canopy and undergrowth came together to form a symphony of the forest; a bird's call; a twig snap; a heart's beat. Delicate skin of fingertips snagged on ragged bark as they curiously traced every curve and cranny. The tallest trees stood burdened with a load of thousands of leaves of varying shades of reds and browns that even the greatest artist could do no justice to.

The smell of rain hung so prominently you could practically taste it. Footsteps indented the soft soil and led further from the humdrum of a busy city and were replaced by the raven's call, the street lights replaced with stars, the smell of exhaust replaced with that of rot. The world was as it should be.

~

Charley Swire's Biography

Charley Swire is 15.

92: THE DEATH OF SUMMER

by Grace Howard

I want light to filter through my eyelashes like lasers of gold. See my Jack Russell dart between the trees, rolling in the fallen leaves that condemned the death of summer.

Let me hear the carefree squeals of my friends when the wind threatened to return our lost inhibitions. Or the call of my mother, "Be careful," to ring through my ears again as the sound of colliding branches battle to outdo her.

Let the smoke from a nearby barbeque pour through my nose and down my throat, or let the fragrance of rose and soil coated in gentle rain take me back.

I want the sweet dew of honeysuckle on the tip of my tongue and the crumble of biscuits between my teeth. The tang of sweets from the corner shop or the saltiness of sweat after a race.

I want my fingers to wrap around the cold chain of a swing while a smooth breeze embraces me, signifying my freedom. I want the sting of grazed knees and dirt beneath my nails again.

~

Grace Howard s Biography

Grace Howard is 15.

93: THE ENERGY CRISIS

by C.I. Selkirk

My heart beat wildly, erratically, faster and faster, until it stopped. The pain in my chest overwhelmed me and I dropped. The floor was cold, hard, and slightly sticky.

Footsteps raced towards me, some clicking, some thudding. Strong hands, the fingernails digging into me, shook my arm. I smelled musk and just-smoked cigarettes, saw blurred shapes and watery colours. Tiny stars appeared and disappeared. My mouth was dry and tasted like old grapefruit and sawdust. A voice, high-pitched and panicked, spoke quickly. Wailing sirens pierced the air, then faded until there was dark silence.

The smell of antiseptic and coffee-breath woke me. The bed was hard and lumpy, the sheets were cool and scratchy. I opened my eyes. The face was translucent white, with bloodshot eyes and three-day-old stubble. My head and stomach hurt and my limbs were weak.

"I don't want to see you in here again," he said, the room swirling around him. "You are an energy drink addict. Get some help." I felt his spittle hit my cheek, hot with disgust.

~

C.I. Selkirk's Biography

No author biography supplied.

94: AND I STILL CAN'T TASTE IT

by Nicole McIntosh

"Let's spring clean," I suggested to my wife.

The look on her face was somewhat displeased. I knew she disliked household chores, but I continued to lay out all the products I could locate in our cleaning cupboard.

"Radio anyone?"

Doing daily boring tasks with no music seemed bizarre, plus the bass beating against the window pane was always encouraging to the ear.

I took the rubbish out and the stench from the communal bin smelt of something I could only describe as death.

The radio helped speed things up and, room by room, we were finished.

Cigarette rolled, yet all I could smell was chlorine.

"My roll-up tastes of bleach," my wife proclaimed.

"What?" I turned to her and took a drag of the orange flamed paper. I waited. I smoked some more until I had only a filter left between my fingers.

"I can't taste it," I said. "I still can't taste it." I sat and thought I now understand the dissatisfaction of spring cleaning and, possibly, smoking.

~

Nicole McIntosh's Biography

Nicole McIntosh is a versatile creative individual making it in the writing world. Having previously written for

True London and attended more than enough writing groups, Nicole is finally writing her own book, *My Friend ADHD*.

Follow her blog for info:
www.tumblr.com/blog/kolewrites

95: THE BAD CATHOLIC (OR, SHERBET LEMON LOVELINESS

by Tracey Maitland

Slowly, I reached into my pocket searching for something safe and familiar. *Why do I have so much rubbish in my pockets?* I thought, as I rummaged through the remnants of old, unused tissues, pen lids and other anonymous paraphernalia. Finally, I felt the smooth, hard surface of the treasure I had been searching for. I stealthily curled my fingers around the hard oval and gently pulled it from my pocket, trying not to make a noise.

Sister Noella glared at me. I froze. When she turned back to the blackboard, I proceeded to pull the two ends apart. The aroma was divine. Lemons filled the air and my anguished mind was transported back to happier times. I slipped the antidote for tedium into my mouth, wrapped my tongue around a little bit of heaven and closed my eyes in ecstasy. Sweetness filled my mouth and fragrance filled my nostrils. All was peaceful for that short, gratifying moment.

"Maitland, what are you eating? Spit it out – it's LENT," demanded Sister Noella. "GOD is watching YOU."

~

Tracey Maitland's Biography

No author biography supplied.

96: GOTH ELEPHANT

by Joseph Hancock

The two of them sat at the black kitchen table which matched the black walls, ceiling, cloths and floor. On the wall was a picture of Nick Cave, dressed in dark grey for a splash of colour.

The three sat quietly over the salty chemical smell of chicken ramen, a one dollar vanilla incense burning on the counter. There was another smell, however, eclipsing the vanilla: chemical soup, the cause of their frustration. Well, that and whose turn it was to empty the cat box sitting a mere five feet away, with a very fresh addition from Bela, their black cat.

It was a standoff as the difficult smell overpowered their ability to enjoy the recently rereleased Joy Division record. Suddenly, the suffocating scent of Aqua-net filled the little room, as another man covered in grey makeup with black eyeliner and lipstick came in.

He took a mouthful of soup and made a face.

"Needs salt," he quipped, then lit a cigarette, the dark angular music filling the polluted air.

~

Joseph Hancock's Biography

Joe Hancock lives in Greenwich, Southern New Jersey, with his dog, Bug. A musician by trade, he is new to the writing field and loving every minute of it.

www.facebook.com/joseph.hancock.9480

97: A SENSE OF LIFE

by Jack Hanlon

Visions of majesty, nature's harmony, the aroma of exotic greenery, contact with new terrain, the zest of unfamiliar delicacies.

All spoilt by your garish shirts, arrogant tone, cheesy footwear, clammy embrace and the lingering staleness of your tobacco kiss.

I stood beside your sickly complexion, listening to your stifled breaths, as your sour scent clogged my throat and you forced me to hold your crusty hand, demanding I swallowed the cake your Mother concocted. I needed to escape.

I have witnessed opportunity, tuned into wise minds, fresh air has entered my lungs, inviting places have met my fingertips, I have sampled freedom. I will never return.

Do not watch your life go by, parroting other people's views, a stagnant stench beneath your nostrils, gripping routine hard, devouring the swill you are fed without protest.

There will never be a limit to the things I want to see, sounds I want to hear, fragrances I want to smell, assets I want to touch and flavours I want to savour.

Goodbye.

~

Jack Hanlon's Biography

All my life I have been telling tales and making up stories. I enjoy reading a diverse mix of genres and incorporating as many as I can into my writing.

I have been lucky enough to see a few of my short stories and poems published and performed at various events.

98: THE SOUND OF WRITING

by Lauren Kearney

A gentle wheeze punctuates the silence, rhythmic and whistling. Cars rumble along the street, occasional snippets of thumping bass creeping through the closed windows.

The wheezing intensifies. It's coming from behind the curtain.

A furious pitter-patter of keyboard keys being struck drowns it out again. For a moment.

Now the huffing starts. Huff, huff, huff, separate to the wheezing. These are the sounds of sleep. The cat dozes behind me, whiskers dancing against rivulets of cigarette smoke. Snuffling and snarking, the dog dreams, the sound mingled like dribbled paint with the clicking and clacking of the keyboard.

Is this what writing always sounds like? Or perhaps, this is the glorious cacophony of procrastination.

~

Lauren Kearney's Biography

Find Lauren on Twitter: @kearneylf

99: KNIGHTS TO REMEMBER

by David Silver

The lights dimmed, the Metro-Goldwyn-Mayer lion roared and Miklos Rozsa's stirring music swirled around the movie's opening credit titles.

The film was *Knights of the Round Table* and what a fabulous battering this schoolboy's senses underwent as he leaned forward excitedly in his front-stalls seat in the autumn of 1954.

Thanks to my purchases from the foyer kiosk, my nostril hairs were already pleasurably tweaked by the salty aroma emanating from a packet of peanuts, and my taste buds set tingling by a tub of vanilla ice cream.

And now, as the feature presentation began, both my vision and hearing were ecstatically assailed by the first Mayer studio movie to use the widescreen process known as Cinemascope and the first international release to feature MGM's new optical track stereophonic sound system.

After the movie was over, I staggered under sensory overload to the cinema manager's office and thanked him for stimulating my sight, hearing, smell and taste.

He smiled and responded, "I'm deeply touched."

~

David Silver's Biography

David Silver was a reporter, sub-editor and columnist on various newspapers in Greater Manchester, England. He retired in 2002 and from 2011-2016 wrote a column for

The Courier, a weekly newspaper for UK expatriates in Spain.

100: SANDY SENSATIONS

by Victoria Simons

The fine golden grains brushed between my toes like the bristles of a slightly stiff brush. My toe nails became combs, cutting through the sand, making swirling psychedelic patterns to mirror the general atmosphere of carefree summertime.

I could almost taste the distinctive tang of sea salt that always clings to your taste buds, even hours after you last felt the cool touch of the clear, glistening water.

Children's laughter tinkled in the distance like high-pitched bells, the air only cheapened by the crass, dissonant tones of the scruffy ice-cream van, piercing the otherwise peaceful ambience.

The sound of the van neared and I awaited the awkward interaction of declining his goods.

The man's voice bellowed, "Ice creams, any flavour. What would you like, love?" The ice-cream van truly was excessive.

The city council's optimistic attempt to bring the seaside inland had been a charming gesture, I thought, as I scraped off as much of the grit from my feet as possible and made my way out of the oversized sandpit.

~

Victoria Simons' Biography

Victoria is an English and Creative Writing student at the University of Warwick. Captivated by the power of the written word, she dreams of using her writing not only for entertainment, but also persuasion, information and generally changing the world.

www.poets.media/authors/victoria-simons

A FINAL NOTE

Allen and I would like to say one last THANK YOU to all the authors featured in this anthology. Their generosity is helping support a very worthy charity and it's an honour to present their stories in this collection.

Don't forget to check my website for more writing challenges – there will be many more appearing in the future. You will be able to find all the details here: www.christopherfielden.com/writing-challenges/

I will say farewell Bristol-style:

Cheers me dears,

Chris Fielden

21748799R00096

Printed in Poland
by Amazon Fulfillment
Poland Sp. z o.o., Wrocław